The Dev-D Syndrome...

Bringing emotional attyachaar to a halt

The Dev-D Syndrome...

Bringing emotional attyachaar to a halt

Chandraprakash Mohata

Srishti
PUBLISHERS & DISTRIBUTORS

Srishti Publishers & Distributors
N-16, C. R. Park
New Delhi 110 019
srishtipublishers@gmail.com

First published by Srishti Publishers & Distributors in 2011

All characters in this book are fictitious, and any resemblance to real persons, living or dead, is coincidental.

Typeset in AGaramond 12pt. by Suresh Kumar Sharma at Srishti

Printed and bound in India

I dedicate
this fiction to the youth
of this country,
who I believe will love me back

Acknowledgements

God, is the one to whom I owe this book. I am neither a professional writer nor an old player in this field. I am a simple human being but what seems special is the Person within me. He is a real Hero for me who made my goal of writing a success. He was the one to believe that I can write and so at every phase of this work he guided me professionally. You know who he is? He is none another than the Almighty.

However, there are certain mortals also who have lent their hand in this story, and they hold an important place in my heart. If it weren't for these people that I thank below, this book would still be languishing in the My Documents folder of the computer.

My readers, you that is, have made me what I am. Thank you for your interest in my work which brought me here to serve you better fiction with years passing by.

My team, MATESZ what I call them, have been the backbone of all my fictions. They might not be literary superpowers, but they always made me feel to have brought the best fiction of my time. In particular I would like to thank:

Ranjani Shastry, the first reader and editor of this book, who have been supporting me with the editorial. She is also the co-founder of the Literature Club Satori - 'let's not yawn' based in Ahmedabad.

Pooja Ugrani, for her wonderful support with the editorials, who has been the hand behind the revision task of this book, which is now in your hand. She is a 23 year old architect from Mumbai.

Apart from her architecture she has been passionate about, reading, writing and editing. Along with her my gratitude to Mr. Ruchir, a literature enthusiast for acting as a love guru and guide me thought the most important chapter of this fiction – *'How to get a girl in 13 days'*.

I am more than happy and thankful to have Akshay Vyas co-founder of House of Ratz for his beautiful cover designing skill, who has brought the best clothes for this breathtaking fiction. This wouldn't have been possible without four of these people.

Pooja, my wife to whom I owe special thanks for being the best companion, standing by the odds and helping me with those wonderful suggestions and comments on the manuscript.

A friend, Philosopher and Guide, Amit Bhatia, who would be my inspiration to write till I die; I owe special thanks to you buddy.

My parents; especially my mom Mulidevi Mohata with Dad Purakhchand Mohata, my brother Manmohan and sister Radha Toshniwal who has been supporting me throughout my life now seems immortal to my eyes. My father-in-law,Ram Ratanji Kothari; for his never ending support and faith in me and his profound belief in *Maji sa*, our holy Goddess and believed that this would become an exclusive piece of fiction for me as an author.

More of a friend than a publisher to me, Srishti has fulfilled my dream by putting his trust in my work and entices people to read my thoughts. He is one of a kind you will rarely find in this world.

I am indebted to that Muse who reflects inside me and always ready with that Mighty pen without whom, my access in this World of Contemporary Writers would not have happened!

Prologue

With the advent of the sun, the darkness experiences a losing battle.

It was indeed a beautiful morning. Weekdays have a certain rhythm of their own but the excitement and craziness of a Saturday or a Sunday stands in direct contrast to a dull orderly Monday.

After a lavish weekend of fun and frolic, the streets are suddenly occupied by grim looking people walking and jogging to their destinations on a Monday morning with one eye on their watches and the other eye on the traffic. The freedom of running in the parks is now enjoyed on the streets as well.

At that point of time when the gates of ATMA opened for the roads to be swept, the sweeper encountered a 'never-seen-before' scenario. A boy lay half dead at the entrance with his hand wounded.

"Oh my God! What has happened to you my child?" the old man cried feeling pity, looking at the condition of the boy lying on the ground. He was wearing denims and a cozy t-shirt smeared with blood; he almost passed off as a local gangster who had tried running away after cheating his Dubai's Don.

The old man shook him again. "Wake up son, look at me!"

Like a concerned father, he tried his best to make the boy regain consciousness. He splashed water on his face but all in vain. It was when he lost hope he decided to call up the boy's family to take responsibility of this poor half dead entity.

"Ahh… hh…!! There is nothing," the man screamed exasperated. He then furiously checked every single pocket of the boy's clothes to search for his identity.

And the thought struck him, “He would at least have his cell phone on him!”

He ransacked every single centimeter of the boy only to find cigarettes and a bottle of alcohol. The boy became a matter of greater concern for the sweeper than his daily chores. Finally after what seemed like hours, the old man thought of calling the ambulance.

SBJ Hospital, Ahmedabad.

8.12 AM, 14th March 2006.

“It’s an emergency! Please...please move aside...!” the clerk shouted in an anxious voice as he was forcing the four wheeled stretcher towards the operation theater.

The condition worsened and the boy needed to be operated urgently. Blood seeped out of his body like rain water from a cracked ceiling, leaving the toughest question for the doctors who stood beside the body to answer; will he survive? They couldn’t find a person who’d sign the guarantee papers for the boy; a circumstance where the common man becomes helpless in the name of law and regulations. Money and rules now became a prime concern considering that boy’s life; it almost felt like a puppet’s show where the strings to the poor boy’s life were being pulled by the rigid rules!

“I don’t know why he is here and what situation brought him here; but at this point he needs to be cured immediately. Don’t you think so? Since he has a broken nerve too?” Dr Astha, a surgeon in the hospital burst out on the authority holders.

"But Doc, we have no authority to proceed. We have to wait until somebody from his family turns up to sign the guarantee papers," replied Dr. Ramesh.

"We can't leave him like this. His life is in danger," she pleaded.

"Let's call Dr Awasthi because here the case demands the police's permission too," Dr. Dushyant suggested from behind.

"What? A po… police case?" She stammered in shock.

"His blood samples are creating a bit of a problem. We have found the presence of cocaine in his blood sample," Dr. Ramesh confirmed showing the lab reports.

"It would be better if the authorities deal with the issue," Dr. Dushyant said with all his politeness.

Dr. Astha, disappointed, gave a nod and took out her cell phone to call.

Tring… tring…

"Hello Dr. Awasthi, good morning. How is your health?"

"Good morning lady. I am pretty fine. What makes you remember this old friend so early today? Any problem?"

"Sir, there is a boy lying in the medical examination room and his condition is serious. Under such a situation when he needs to be operated immediately is it necessary to fulfill the formality of paperwork before we start working on him?"

"What has happened to him?" He questioned.

"A broken nerve with cocaine in his blood sample," she uttered hesitantly in a low tone. Astha knew that this fact will sink her ship of expectations.

"He is a drug addict; we cannot interfere. It's better to shift him to some government hospital."

"But Sir, he has no time!"

"I can understand, Dr. Astha, how you might be feeling but we cannot proceed unless somebody from the boy's family comes. Hundreds of patients come to a hospital like this; we cannot cure everyone for free."

"Sir…!" She pleaded again.

While Dr. Awasthi got a reason to skip providing free benefits; Dr. Astha made a decision which nobody in their wildest dreams would have ever thought of.

"Sir, I respect your words but under this situation, when there is nobody to take care of the boy I would like to sign the guarantee papers. The police can even do their work after the treatment."

"Why the hell do you want to take this on your head Dr. Astha? Don't you realize the danger you are putting yourself into? I am also a human like you and can understand your compassion. But I have a better solution for you," he said.

"What solution are you offering Sir?"

"The press is the best possible way out of such a crisis. Somebody will turn up for sure after reading the newspaper. Till then you can start working on him on an official basis."

"That's a good idea! Thank a ton, Doc!" Dr. Astha said and hung up the phone heaving a sigh of relief.

~

When you get up early in the morning, what do you generally expect?

A good morning tea or maybe the sunlight pouring into your room or a face that makes you smile.

I expect the morning paper on my table folded in such a way that the front page is always visible; but what I saw on the front page that day left me speechless.

Sheena was sitting beside me. I screamed throwing the paper as if I had seen a ghost on it. Horror and shock were emotions that could be seen on my face. She asked me twice, shaking me hard asking me again and again as to what had happened; but I couldn't utter a single word. I had lost my voice somewhere in the depths of my throat.

There were questions written all over her face, but I wasn't in a position to answer any of those. It felt like a stab deep in my heart. I couldn't just be sitting on the sofa after seeing a half-dead Sid with blood smeared all over his face staring at me from the front of page of the morning paper.

Running to my room I grabbed a t-shirt. Sheena asked where I was going; but at that point of time I had no fake reasons to give her.

What would I have said? That our dear friend is dying? The only best friend that we had is lying somewhere on a hospital bed covered with blood?

I rushed to the hospital asking for the face which had come in today's newspaper. Sid was a brother to me; not by blood but by relation and I had been missing him since the last two days. After a frantic search of every corner of the hospital, I found him lying on a stretcher. I would never have imagined Sid to be in such a situation. I tried to reach him but was stopped by two ward boys outside.

“Leave me please! The person inside is my best friend. I want to see him urgently!”

My plea did not have any effect on their stone hearts but Dr. Astha came to the rescue all of a sudden, on hearing our loud argument outside her office. On understanding what was going on, she took me inside.

“What’s the matter? What happened to Sid?” I questioned.

“So you are his brother?” Dr. Astha pulled her stethoscope away from Sid’s narrow chest and adjusted her pink shirt.

“Doctor, I’m his friend and he is an orphan. Is there anything serious?”

“Everything is serious around here. I would like to draw some blood samples and run a few tests,” she said as she signaled a nurse, who came in with her tray, syringe, vials and her rubber tourniquet.

Dr. Astha laid him down on the examination table and asked me to hold his shoulders. I watched the needle pierce into the fair skin of his arm.

I waited for the results of the blood test outside her office. It was almost an hour before Dr. Astha called me in again.

“Sid’s tests are a little problematic,” she said. “We did a series of tests and have gradually found out that Sid’s FVC ratio has fallen below 75% and has caused an isolated reduction in the red blood cells.”

I tried to remember what the red blood cells do in our bodies.

“I am sorry to give you this bad news but your friend is suffering from COPD,” she said in a low whisper.

"C..O..P..D.." I only stared at her with fixed eyes. "What does that mean?"

"To put it in simple words, he is suffering from Chronic Obstructive Pulmonary Disease which is related to lung cancer," she said.

I shook my head. I had been at the hospital for the last one hour and with every passing minute it got more difficult to believe that Dr. Astha had made a mistake. I waited for some divine intervention to take place; I wished that Dr. Astha would assure me that the report was not his but somebody clse's and that there was nothing to worry about. I hoped that she might be kidding. But instead, I watched my own hands move of their own accord to take the piece of paper which Dr. Astha offered.

It was written, "Damage to the alveoli (air sacs) has blocked the airflow and has caused emphysema."

At that moment, I cursed myself for choosing the commerce stream over science.

My tongue felt as heavy as lead with the weight of the question that I was forced to ask, "Is he going to die?"

"COPD has no cure yet. However, treatments and an appropriate lifestyle can help Sid feel better; he needs to engage himself in healthy activities and quit smoking which will retard the progress of the disease. Once he quits, the degradation of his lungs will slow down considerably."

I pushed the technical words out of my head and instead, sunk my teeth to the one sentence that gave me hope; Sid needed to quit smoking to live. "Is there a treatment?" I asked.

"Yes. With aggressive treatment, COPD carries a survival prognosis of nine months to three years," the doctor leaned forward showing me sympathy. "But..."

"But what doctor?" I questioned.

"The disease that he is suffering from will make it hard for him to breathe. He may die anytime due to a heart attack."

Her words gave me a shiver and I couldn't hold back that tear coming out of my eye.

"Listen... what's your name?"

"It's Dev...Devendra Rai!"

"I just wanted to know a few things about Sid for which it will need your co-operation," Astha said.

"But can you tell me why any of this is important?"

"It's just for medical history. But to be frank, I personally want to know everything I can about Sid, so that I can understand the reason he has reached this condition today."

"He is my room-mate in college and has got all evens with just one odd; he is addicted to smoking."

"You know something? He resembles my son who too suffered from COPD."

"Oh... I'm so sorry," I said.

"I couldn't save his life, but I will not let Sid die," a tear slid down her eyes too and fell on the table. "Was Sid in love with somebody?"

Some stories are written in blood and Sid's story always gave a hint of that. It was a girl, who was the burning vital flame of his life.

Now fire's a beautiful thing; something you can't take your eyes off, when it's burning. If you keep it contained, it will serve you light and heat; but once left lose it can take over the strongest people. Like they say, fire's a humble servant but a terrible master. He got her taste; a taste which wasn't meant for him.

I sat in silence for a few moments, thinking about everything I had just said. Sometimes I wondered what would've happened if I had never met him; never ventured down that unknown vast tarred path of mystery. Would destiny have brought us together still?

All I could do was think; think about what could've happened, if I had done the right thing or had made the right decision. If I had known of this future, would I have it changed?

My mind reflected a turbulent sea as these thoughts and questions kept coming to me. There were so many things unknown to me. They were questions that required an abundant amount of thought, which made me come out of my comfort zone and relive certain past events that were better left forgotten!

"You look very tensed dear. Speak out what is inside; it will make you feel light."

"I have only known him for three years. But if you took every memory, every moment that I spent with him and if you stretch them end-to-end, they would last forever. That's how special he is to me."

"This is happening because I didn't listen to him. He pleaded to me to understand how much he loved that girl; but I never took him seriously. This is happening because I just wanted to get him out of all the mess he had put himself into.

This is happening because I did not realize how good I would eventually be."

A guilt developed inside me as I visualized my fate. "It's me who is responsible for all this," I shouted in pain.

"But why do you think it's you?" she placed her hand on my shoulder in sympathy.

"I must have done something bad when I was younger for fate to have played this cruel trick on me," I said, bemused.

My eyes filled up with tears and they started streaking my face. "For weeks, I mulled over what wrong I had done to deserve this kind of life. Was I a bad friend? Perhaps, I did hurt someone intentionally for the sake of friendship and now I was paying for it? Doubting myself and my character, I fell into a deep depression and no one could get me out of it. I was so ashamed of being such a failure!"

"Please tell me what actually happened," she asked while consoling me to speak out the thing that was causing such pain inside me, to snap me out of the depression. She was determined to learn from all the painful events that had happened to Sid & me recently. Maybe, coz she knew that life had its own seasons, and that there might be a similar rainy day for her too.

I wondered why Dr. Astha was holding onto all the painful events and wallow in self-pity. What did she expect to learn from them? Those memories could only make her cry; she needed to move on.

"Do you know Doctor why a person misses somebody?

It's when you have enjoyed the best moments of your life with him and when you need 'the him' again, his absence creates a vacuum in our heart."

"Why? What happened? Any quarrel between you?"

"It's a long story. Leave it."

"No I want to listen," she interrupted.

Finally, taking a deep breath and I began to speak.

1

It was drizzling and the night had fallen. The wind was slowly turning stormy and the roads were almost wet. Pitter-patter of the rain was the only sound, that evening apart from the sound of the burning gas stove from a tea stall a few meters away. The rain must have helped the *chai wala* in anticipating unusual profit margins contributed by his beloved customers. I looked at the new Titan that showed half past seven which I got as Gift from Pooja on my last Birthday.

I waited behind the red bungalow for her that was diagonally opposite to the barren land which was located at the rear side of the tea stall on the lane. Tea stall faced the main road. This half lit lane by the sepia lights led to her house. Thanks to the Corporation for lights with less voltage. The rain cooled the atmosphere and I was shivering.

She could predict few things. One, the next morning news will be announcing 'a heavy rain last night' and the other that I would hardly be ready to leave the place without seeing her face and exchanging few words. What could she possibly do? Though I belonged to a middle class, Pooja had fallen for my masculine charms and my athletic build. Besides she never believed in discrimination. Alas! The drizzle has turned into steady rain. She could either meet me behind the red bungalow or sit back into the comforts of her home before anyone realizes her absence in the house. It was a tough call to make. There was a debate of mental impulse and heartfelt warmth inside her. The girl chose her heart. The rain was God's way of testing her - she thought, and she was determined not to fail. Not this time. I waved my hand in delight as I saw her. Taking long strides, she smiled to brag about her brilliancy in taking a 'wise' decision.

She checked her watch and showed me her palm indicating 'five'. Hope they would have meant hours but I knew it was just, "five minutes of gain with two minutes of pain". She never understood my phrases. But then I was always like that - using phrases which never made any sense to her.

At that point of time nothing could have made any sense to her because she knew that she was in the safest arms of this universe. No sooner her hands were over the sides of my neck. I held her from the waist and her wet locks fell on my fingers caressing through her shoulders. I wished the shoulders were mine.

I asked, "Why did you get so late?"

She kept mum.

It was still 'love in the rains' or 'Loving the rains'.

I went closer to please her rosy lips. I felt her warmth and to give way to our lust…

BEEPED – THE NON LIVING 'MAN MADE'

The shrill ringing pierced the silence of my room. It was that stupid alarm which disturbed like the ability to make sounds of snore gifted to a fat man. It was almost done this time. But damn it! This time it was the wonderfully manufactured Alarm Clock. Actually, last time she didn't even turned up so this time I was much angry on that stupid clock. I groaned again as I tossed left to right while covering my ears with my pillow. More you press your head with the pillow the louder the buzz gets in the pink ears. I closed my eyes tightly, getting annoyed at the sound of the early riser!

Beep... Beep... Beep…ppp

I wanted to smash the alarm so bad but it wasn't the unique human being. Though I could break it this Morning, but my parents would still buy me another one! It was like a torture. The drowsiness made the body hard to even lift itself. It lasted only for few seconds before my hand collide with the annoying electronic, patting it to be silence immediately. Cold bit at my exposed hands in air outside the blanket and I quickly returned it under the safe shelters of my warm blanket.

23rd June, 2003. 3.00 AM

I thought the Sun must be waiting for his clock to strike round about six as usual. What a monotonous schedule he goes through?

Rising from the same direction every time and, then setting in the West. I wonder what he would have written on the social networking site – connecting through satellites before the Moon could comment

-'You are Lucky, Sun! I always have to be standing in the dark and it is very cold in winters too.'

I stared up at the sky admiring its beauty.

"Stupid Alarm Clock" I complained to none but the walls while entering to my bathroom. I looked at myself in the mirror, poking and prodding, examining my face. A bath was urgently required.

Within minutes I got ready. I wore formal clothes for an executive look as if they were going to give me the admission, looking at my attire. I was going to stand in a queue for my admission at IMS, Ahmedabad.

Scholars from all over the nation were going to land here. After school, it's every student wish to get inside a leading institute. It's a career defining stage and you come down to a stage of decision making. Though I scored 82 percent in the higher secondary certificate, I wasn't assured of getting a seat in this college to set my eyes before the walls that were painted with quotes by great men. But I wondered why sentences spoken by women are not quoted often like that of men.

Of course seats were limited and I was surely not the only scholarly person who scored above eighty percent. For the first time in my life I was so tensed that sweat made me bath twice. Mom was already in the kitchen ready to put hot pan on stove after preparing the dough for the fried snacks. Grey haired Dad wiping his spectacles, in front of the old antique mirror with exquisite teak wood frames that had the capacity to show you how both your limbs look like apart from your face and torso.

"O maa… Pup-paa, Morning!" I chipped the silence coming down the stairs.

"Yes! Come, Good Morning, beta. Don't forget any of your papers today.

(After a pause)

"Y-o-u Dev. I am not speaking to any body else," dad said moving away his head towards me.

As soon as I nodded with a sigh, a sweet aroma from the air that filled my nostrils made me more comfortable. This clueless gaseous molecules scattered around me seemed to keep me in much comforted position for no reason than the organized piece of an advice from the man wearing the neatly wiped spectacles.

I turned and discovered that it was the smell of the Lilac flavored Agarbatti and not that dream girl Pooja.

"Aha… She also smells the same many time," I thought aloud.

"Who smells like what? To whom are you talking with, Dev," my Father turned his eye balls piercing through the glasses towards his son dressed like a gentleman.

"Oops… He had overheard it." I thought to myself and I tried shifting his attention from such a focal Point.

"Uh, nothing dad, but tell me, are you coming over breakfast with me?"

"I think so. He will", my mother continued, "What would you have, Ji?"

"Home made Parathas with pasteurized Milk's Curd" I said politely with eyes on my plate that contained a hot steaming Paratha.

"Did she ask you?" My dad poked me on my interruption.

"Because, I guess there is nothing else that she can serve her husband this morning, Sir!" I laughed.

My mother pulled my ears tagging me naughty.

"What Chemistry!" I spitted. *"Abhi to mein jawan hu…"* I tuned my vocal on those lyrics.

"Should I add your favorite butter and spice over it, Dev?" She winked at me least bothered about the calories she was offering. I had no other choice except water my mouth on a spoonful of exported quality yellow peanut butter. I chuckled exchanging few glances with her.

She acted pretty much like my peer, not childish, but jovial. I always kept telling myself that she was elder to me but then nothing seems to create a difference between us. I washed hands and I dumped the duly filled admission forms and necessary documents required. The drive was about two hours in absence of traffools (traffic fools).

Vroom………… Went my Zen!

Father spits out his Surprise saying, "I don't even believe my ears how I was convinced by your daughter, Mrs. Rai.

Mummy answered, “Yes, Dev’s Daddy, I guess my daughter can convince the Prime Minister too!”

I giggled, “Paa, Maa is absolutely right! She can even use her powers to change the Government if she can convince a stern disciplinarian father like you.” I said while Mother India just passed frequent grins.

My sweet sister Tullika held a magic rod that she inherited from the same womb from where I also came. At that juncture of Green signal from big daddy, I was elated beyond words. I wish somebody tells me how I should feel – A happy lad because I was going to be free or a sad painted face as I was leaving home and its comforts.

At last my happiness overshadowed my sorrow. I was all geared up and packing bags and bags to be carried and finally I was off to the hostel. Like others’ wandering mind I also was nagged by a silly thought on and off. It was about making friends in Ahmedabad. I was equally thrilled, though the thought of leaving my loving, aging parents left me melted inside.

My birth place was ‘Nadiad’, a small town and I couldn’t think of spending my whole life there. The kind of orthodox people that prevailed there always blocked me from achieving great heights. Post-graduation was on my chart but it was dad who wanted an early retirement. On the other hand Jasoda aunty and Ram uncle had different plans for me. Oh! They were planning me to bind in the wedlock with their only daughter and handle their provision store to me as dowry to be taken care.

I mumbled, “I am not a sellable product in the name of a bride groom?!”

My great plans were the only hope which I had and its fulfillment was a must. IMS was not only good one but the Best among many in the city that gave personal attention to their student. Along with studies, they provided all aids to fulfill dreams that I was passionate about. Talents got stage to showcase them.

I was going to have a brand new academic life, novel friends, and an attitude to adopt, and maybe a girlfriend! Thoughts occupied the route I traced to reach college. Mom and dad bid adieu after dropping me at the gate. The institute seemed like one we always see in Mukesh bhatt’s horror flicks. Still there was enough time. I was quite early unlike every time.

Pressurized by the nature’s call I had to rush to the Loo... My feet moved in to the 6X8 wash room titled “Gents” situated on the second floor of IMS. And my luck saw a guy walk-in at the same moment who seemed pissed off before really pissing off!

Uff... I Pity the beast! He was wearing faded jeans hung low, but unlike the men displaying their branded inners of few hundred Bugs! His Red shirt was tucked in loosely at the Collar to appeal the ‘V’ Neck Lady lover! I gazed to check his appearance. He was just heart throbbing, not less than a ‘Macho man’. Can I now say- Extremely Beautiful? I never thought I’d ever use that term for a wannabe like him at least, but there was just something so devout about him which aroused jealousy in guys! Oh... Now you should decipher the depth of the word 'Beautiful'?

"Hey this is Dev," I initiated the conversation.

Hi I'm Sid…Dev?

A few seconds of silence prevailed but then he suddenly started to whistle. I wondered if he had liters inside to pore out. I too joined him with his *Dil to Pagal hai* tune. While we were busy mingling, I saw a one-liner written on the wall. Sid too saw and read it loudly, "*Don't look down … that really stinks.*" His laughter filled my ears and my own laugh escaped.

Some people meet accidentally in restaurants, some in park or movie theaters. You always remember the first place when you meet an interesting person but where I met him was not a place to remember at all. But that joke acted as a tiny seed, which God planted to grow a relation named friendship.

Strangers do not need an introduction to smile, they just need a moment to share and then pass on. But for us that moment acted as a connecting link. We came out of that Important Place mingling together but then our eyes got surprised when we found a long queue already formed in front of the counter to fill the forms and get admitted.

"Shit! How come these assholes popped up all of a sudden?" Sid thought aloud in despair. It seemed like a surprise party organized for us and we, duo, were birthday boys. Taking our grim looking faces, we stood at the back with hundreds of mother fuckers ahead. The possibility of getting admission now turned to least.

The clock showed 6am which meant another two hours for

admission window to open. I felt like I was in the queue waiting to buy a Blockbuster movie ticket. I stared at Sid with all hopes as if he would really act as a Genie.

"What?" Sid shouted when he found me staring at him every now and then. I was looking at him to get the solution because my mind had stopped answering.

"You got something inside your brains" I said.

"Why can't you go back to the loo. Good ideas generates faster there with no ill thoughts", he replied.

"Dude! Imagine I am that hot 36 24 36, long hairs with short wears, won't you come to rescue of the pretty lady? Hunh! Answer me…?"

"Everything seems thirty-six over here" he laughed.

Excuse me guys! This was my place, "*Aain… Hun Ubhe-tti,*" a girl with that typical *khaman - Undhiyu* accent interrupted.

"Oh I am so sorry! You first," I allowed her to stand in front. By the way I am Dev – Devendra Rai"

"I am Sheena Patel. Good to know that… and Thanks too!"

"For what?" I inquired.

"Well somethings don't need a reason but when you have asked, why I did, will tell you some other day if we manage to get inside this college"

"Is she your sister?" Sid asked.

"Thank God… She isn't," I giggled.

"Then why the fuck you believed that she was in front"

"Does that make a difference as the admission criteria already sucks, Dude?

If she gets in, then we too will make it to the ramp!"

"You the big 'D'- D-e-v-e-n-d-r-a Rai, What if she is the last one?"

"That sounds much better than we too fighting for a single seat if we were at last."

"Hey Dev! Won't you introduce your friend who isn't happy with me?"

"So you make people happy"

"Not that way what your shitty mind is thinking about"

"Guys, I have a plan if you are with me," I said.

"A plan"? What plan are you talking about? Are you making a plan for her to make me happy?

It took seconds for me to grab attention of the crowd and slowly break the line to crooked strait! I did pinch Sheena with all my guts. I enjoyed playing the Drama after long time…

"You asshole what you did with my girl", I shouted at Sid holding his collar.

Sid seemed shocked at this sudden reaction of mine. He checked my eyes.

If I was kidding him…

'What, what did…? I do?", He voiced reality.

"Yeah! He did pinch me at the waist," Sheena affirmed pointing at her still bulging waist.

"Who will pamper this fat lady," Sid screamed.

"Fuck you scoundrel," I said and blew a punch at Sid's pretty white nose. He caught my left eye blink. And then he started to spread the chaos in corner with his fake punches in air. Soon the mess started into a fight. A punch from me and Sid fell on the people standing in the queue.

In such fights, you might find more of viewers taking utmost pleasure of the live show without even caring for what they have been fighting or who were they fighting, unless you are of a great concern to the crowd. We almost came in front fighting with each other with Sheena gathering sympathy from onlookers, especially boys who were standing. She almost made them push behind. The queue became a chaos of grim looking people standing all together as crowd. May be they wanted to make themselves safe but they were least aware of the damage this *'Rajnikant' dhishoom... Dhishum styles* would be doing to the Fans of fighters like me and Sid. Looking at the rowdy behaviors, the security guards rushed to stop the mess we were creating. I gestured Sheena to catch the right place. Even the professors and other staff members turned up to get the situation in control.

"Leave me, I want to smash him", Sid urged struggling to escape from that security guards hands.

"Come outside mother fucker, I will show you the darker side of

Dev," struggling to sound as loud as he was, I tried to threaten that handsome.

The faculties, thinking it would be wise to interfere, took control of the situation! They requested us to calm down indicating the guards to leave us in freedom. But that wasn't done with, because one of the professors thought for a happy ending for us.

"Why were you fighting like dogs?"

"Sir, he pinched my girlfriend and no boy would have liked this. Imagine if it was your girl, how would you feel Sir? Tell me…" I said.

The disgusted Professor could do nothing but to frown at me as if I have disclosed his sexual affairs with his maid which are usually supposed to be under the carpet.

"I am sorry to intervene before you speak," Sid started to clarify. I didn't do anything, Sir. Honestly… Believe me… My bag just passed her and she mis-interpreted it as if I touched her. Unnecessarily, she busted out. If this lady still thinks of me behaving this way, then I strongly make an apology, kneeling down"

And he kept his words. He did kneel down.

"Nautanki sa… la…" my mind spitted controlling shrill laugh. His drama made him an innocent being and now it was my turn to prove my innocence.

"You didn't do…?" I passed a soft gasp to be as polite as I could.

"No... Not at all," he clarified.

"Oh I'm so sorry brother I punched you like a boxer. You can understand the criticality of carrying a girlfriend," I picked up Sid from his shoulders to make his stand. He hugged me so tightly like lord Rama did in Ramayan to his brother Bharat when they met while in 'Exile'. The chaos at IMS clapped in appraisal to watch a happy ending in front of its eyes. One who was in the queue, as a victim of this drama, must have definitely thought this was even better than K3G! But they didn't know which master minds have been working behind the drama. It was quite late for them to realize that when the gates of the building for admission opened, they had lost the places they reserved in the line. The people pushed each other to release their anguish.

Finally, we got the seat for our deserving asses but Sheena passed shrill laughs every now and then until we departed back towards home.

College…! It's a whirlwind. Your parents tell you not to bunk, don't smoke, don't consume alcohol, don't get a girl pregnant, study well and finally, "make us proud." Then they hug you and with tears in their eyes, watch you fly away from the nest.

I was the same free bird, free to roam, from my nest and get my dreams fulfilled. It was the enrollment day and I was all set to move with the fact that I was moving to college permanently for three years, it became the most exciting moment of my life.

I was moving in today into my new hostel, and I was looking forward to this day but I just didn't know what to expect out of it, and question began popping in my head thinking what it be like? Was college going to be fun? Was my roommate going to be Sid? Is my hostel room pretty or a junkyard? Will I meet new people?"

Thoughts didn't leave my mind until we reached IMS. Once my dad found a place to park I got out of the car to get my suitcases from the back of the car.

This was the best college in Ahmedabad and was consistently ranked seventh all over the country. My mouth left open looking at the chicks around. This made me slightly comfortable because I had lots of choices. I saw girls with every bust size possible.

I thanked god to have given me such a chance to explore mankind. I stood by the hostel gate pitying the jeans worn by such women when suddenly my mom snapped me out of my reverie.

"What are you doing?" she said giving that eagle's eye.

"Nothing", I said as I went to reach for my heavy suitcase loaded with mom's love.

"Put down kid", my dad shouted.

"Dad I have grown up now", I said ignoring him and reached for a bigger luggage. I searched my jeans to get a folded piece of paper that had the information on my receipt number. We moved our feet's towards the reception with my thoughts getting deeper and deeper about me living in hostel.

I sighed again. My arms and legs were cramping and my suitcase felt heavier than usual. Finally, after what seemed like an hour, we reached the end of the hall and stood in front of a door written "Office" and knocked.

"Come in", someone responded so I opened the door and looked inside.

There was a large sofa with a coffee table and a lady sitting at a desk reading some documents. She looked old, old enough to be a grandmother. She reminded me of fat ass Jasoda aunty who got white hairs all over her head and also got a visible mustache.

The clock read 04.35 pm. The lady smiled at me and so I smiled back. For moments we repeated the same act but then, "Can I be of any assistance", she asked.

"I'm Devendra Rai! Could you check my registration please", I offered her my receipt number for her ease.

She looked at the paper on her desk. There was silence for a whole minute. While she searched for my name, I got a chance to put my bags down and stretch my arms. It felt good so good.

'Well here is your room number and keys. College starts on Monday and here is your routine,' she said handing me the stuff.

'Thanks,' I said.

I picked up my bags and walked to the door when the lady said, 'why are you so late, you should have been here by noon?

'Actually my dad got lost", I smiled weakly pinpointing his high powered spectacles.

I looked down at my room key. It said 314. I climbed almost sixty stairs, walked all the way down the hall and down another one and I finally stopped in front of the very last room. By now, I was so tired; I could just collapse on the floor.

There was a piece of card attached to the key.

I looked at the card and shouted in joy. It said, Devendra Rai & Sid Agrawal. My happiness crossed all limits when I got my wish come true.

My parents began to help me in setting up my stuff like clothes and other stuffs. It took about an hour and a half to set. I locked my Elmira with a heavy metal bar. Now as time passed I began getting curious to see Sid. My parents wanted to see him too so we decided to kill time and go out for dinner. By the time we finished it was 8:45. Sid's visibility was doubtful. My parents still had a long ride back home so they decided to meet my roommate later.

I hugged my mom and she departed with my father back home leaving me behind. I rushed to my room to check whether Sid has arrived or not.

As I entered the room.

"Who are you?" is all she could say in a sour tone. She got so mad that she started screaming like anything, and what made it worst is, she just had a towel on with bikini's hanging on the wall. I looked at her. She was damn beautiful with chiseled features, high cheekbones and overgrown hair.

"Who are you?!" she banged this time with a bit more aggressive.

"I'm your new roommate" I said smiling as if she was really my roommate.

I wondered how she got the keys but then it all seemed understood. The girls hostel was situated on the left and boy's one on the right with same room numbers. The lady at the office might have delivered Sid's key to her. I was much sure about my room as it has our name engraved on the key.

Her eyes widened, "y-you're..... My what!?" she started to feel light head with all the emotions: from stupid, to angry, to embarrass, to confused. This was not something she might have expected.

"I'm...your...roommate" I said it while standing up to tease her more. She got into a wrong room was something I had discovered quiet earlier but needless I thought not to disclose.

"I know what you said, what I'm trying to get out... is why? I've never signed up for co-ed room and why are you looking at me? And at my stuff? Her towel slid down a bit.

She closed her eyes hoping I didn't pay attention to that, but it was I who had to close the eyes. I let out a loud laugh through my lips. "I liked it better when you were aggressive", I said.

"You are such a jerk" she said and began walking away to the direction out of my room.

"Where are you going" I asked being shocked.

"Too the office with a charge on you for molesting me" she said giving me a smirk.

"Have you gone insane?" I shouted throwing her stuff out of the room. First it's my room with Dev & Sid engraved on the keys and second wear something before you move with no clothes.

"Just… keep your mouth shut!" she boiled on me.

I playfully zippered my mouth, locked it and shoved an invisible key in my pocket.

"Can you be less dramatic?" she said then got into my handsome face where we were only inches away and I noticed she had blue eyes that were out of this world.

"What did you say?"

"Less... dramatic...! You just took my stuff out of the room that I picked and you took it without asking, how I am supposed to react?" she said.

"Well, you took the room without asking either?"

"Don't turn it around on me" she busted while gathering her things. You should have acted like a gentleman which you're certainly not."

I grabbed her arm to stop and looked straight into her eyes. She had anger on her adorable face, like she would kill me someday, "And you're not acting very lady like either" and the mood turned into an angry nod.

We stared at each other for a moment, and she stayed composed trying to give the angriest look she could.

I don't know why it's scientific but you always dream of what remains unsaid lying beneath your heart. Yes I did dream for that girl and I gradually realized she would love me some day. I felt sorry for the mischief I played with that girl but then it was just what I felt.

2

The sunlight spilled over my blanket, but it still wasn't morning for me.

The morning rays of the sun felt like a smooth silk cloth gently moving over my skin, caressing me. I'm not a very morning person so, like most of you, I found it very, very frustrating to get up from bed. I saw the time. It said 6a.m. I yawned and settled in for a five minute snooze. The next thing I knew, Sid was shaking me, yelling in my ears to get up for class.

I looked at the clock - 7a.m. Bull shit! I had slept for another whole hour! I mumbled.

I jumped out of my bed and ran to the bathroom to do the morning necessities while Sid got my breakfast. I thought to give mess hygiene a check late by night and rush to class immediately. All I could do was gulping it down while rushing to class. While the two of us were running,

"*Hey Bhagwan*! I can't believe I lost 300 grams!" This loud exclamation of losing 300 grams was made by none other than Miss Sheena. She was a perky girl with one major problem; she was happily over weight.

Let me have the pleasure of introducing this 'sweet like saccharine' lady, Sheena Patel, who belonged to a traditional Indian family where only arrange marriages got a nod and people in such contexts seemed a little narrow-minded in their thoughts. However, Sheena's parents were quite an antithesis when it came to adhering to societal norms i.e. they were extremely cool. They gave good space to their children to pursue whatever they liked, yet they were very traditionally rooted. She too like me was born and brought up in the outskirts of the city Ahmedabad, somewhere near *Kutch* and her life turned 360 degrees when she got a chance to study in a city called Ahmedabad. The only thing that kept her worried was her parents' extra caring nature. She had an inferiority complex that generally affects many overweight girls. So while her parents didn't bother about her obesity, she too got this 'I don't give a damn about my weight' attitude. According to her belief, obese people were the most jovial human beings to be with and the never-say-die spirit was present in huge quantities inside them. So what if they don't find clothes of their size at the normal stores? There is always an ice cream parlour to get over the shortcoming with an ice-cream.

"Waaoo... Congratulations, girl! If you thought you were the only fat ass lass in the world, then you were so fucking mistaken."

"Oh..! Is it?" Sheena grinned.

"Finally you can update your Facebook status again," said Jasmeet, her new friend in college. Jasmeet was the one whom I had seen clothed only in a towel in my room last night.

Jasmeet, the *Punjabi kudi* from Panipat came all the way from a place known for its royal heritage, history and food. She came from a nuclear family and so the care and comfort she got from her parents reflected in her lifestyle. She was mommy's girl and so her anger, ego and attitude couldn't spare anyone. Her parents were initially skeptical of sending her to IMS; Sonepat was nearby, convenient (In case you are geographically lost, please Google it up) and the quality of education was also quite good. She never wanted to go against her family but Sonepat was not the place she had imagined as her future destination. Finally, she had managed to reach IMS, all thanks to her elder sister whose efforts had brought Jasmeet into a new world of endless possibilities.

There were things in common between these two members of the fairer sex; both of them were a little esoteric in their own style and they also happened to be roommates.

The first period was Economics.

Sid and I grabbed the second row chairs beside Jasmeet. She was engrossed in a book with the title 'Principles of Economics'. Her blue eyes (which I discovered were the effect of the Lomb lenses) moved from side to side, faster than I thought was ever possible. When she looked at me, a wave of the salty azure ocean crashed on me. They suited her and were indeed beautiful. But that anger that burst out of her almost instantly at all times, spoiled all the exquisiteness.

The teacher walked in.

"Hello class. My name is Fatima, and I'll be taking Economics for you this year," she said and turned around facing the green board to write down something.

In the classroom, a lot of general whispering was going on. At that moment, a girl walked in. She was wearing a green and blue shade dress. Her hair was in a messy ponytail tied high up above the medulla oblongata. She was looking at the professor with a smiling face. She looked so happy and peaceful; like nothing could ruin that moment.

"Ah...! Tehzeeb, am I right?" asked Miss Fatima.

She nodded looking at her. You cannot deny the fact about some females belonging to the Islamic culture, that they have beautiful chiseled features. They are fair, pink lips, deep black eyes the size of chick peas behind a mysterious veil showering extra charm at all times as if waiting to see their 'better halves' just after the magical words are spoken thrice – *'Kabool hai, Kabool hai, Kabool hai'*. However, Tehzeeb did look different from her classmates. She didn't follow the *purdah* system.

"Well then, welcome to your first class at IMS. Please take a seat so that we can start." The Professor's voice interrupted my 'in-depth' analysis of Miss Tehzeeb.

She nodded again and looked directly at Sid. He blushed and quickly looked away realizing that he was gawking at her.

"Hey...Can I sit here?" she asked Sid pointing to the empty seat next to him.

It felt as if world stopped for Sid. His heart started beating crazy and I could easily hear the pounding. I gave a jerk but he seemed to have lost into the beauty of that girl he had just seen. I had to nudge him, waking him from the dream he was watching and I couldn't, for God's sake, understand 'Why?' and 'How come so soon?' He went absolutely blank. I advised him to calm down but something serious seemed to occupy his mind.

"Umm...yes?" He said, but that sounded like a question.

"Look I understand if you have a problem," she began but was cut off by a girl's yelling.

"Hey Tehzeeb," yelled Sheena waving her hands frantically trying to draw her attention. "Come sit here," she said pointing the seat next to her. This was something special about Sheena. She had no apprehensions about meeting new people and adjusting herself like a liquid poured in various shaped beakers. Things were quite different for her perky roommate Jasmeet who could never forget the way we met.

"Oh...okay!" said Tehzeeb walking over to her.

Sid went slumped on his seat.

"Great, just fucking great! She came over and I couldn't even talk to her properly."

"But dude why the hell are you feeling so bad? Brother you are going insane," I said.

"It's a matter to feel bad! Just 5 minutes ago my life got changed; it was because of her. That girl, who was going to sit right next to me, for some reason, I couldn't even breathe when I saw her. The clock stopped for a while and I could only see her in the classroom," he said. I could only gawk at Sid with bare eyes on looking at his expressions, while he kept venting out his *filmi thoughts*.

"Get out of here, you two," a loud screeching voice entered our ears when we saw the professor standing in front of us pointing towards the door to make an exit.

It was sheer feeling of shame for me that we were thrown out of the class by the professor on the very first day of college.

Sid asked me to join for some *samosas*. On the way he continued his rant over and over again.

"Believe me dude she looked so good! Gosh…damn sexy, any guy would have fallen head over heels for her. I can't believe God was hiding this beauty from me for the last 20 years of my life!"

"But you are just nineteen!"

"How can you forget those nine months of life in exile?" he reminded me.

"Her curly hair, those full pink lips, and her eyes...O my dear God, her eyes... My skin boiled, my face heated up, I could feel the sweat forming at the back of my neck, my throat closing up, damn, who was this girl; an *Apsara* from the kingdom of Lord Indra? I did not believe in love at first sight; well that was before I met her."

"OMG..." my jaw dropped in astonishment. What the hell was happening here?

"What the fuck are you speaking man? I thought you were going insane; now I know you actually are." It was our first day with the first lecture still going on and Siddharth Agrawal wanted me to believe this stupid thought that he was actually in love with a girl; who could be anything from bi-sexual to homo-sexual.

The discussion went on and on until Sid finally made me realize that the girl, whom he has just seen, now meant the world to him.

The two of us went to the canteen and ended up having a lot more than just *samosas.*

As we walked in silence, I stopped suddenly. Something weird was happening inside me. Since when did I start getting butterflies in my stomach? I wondered what had triggered this. I had never felt like this before. The butterflies fluttered some more in my stomach as I raced my brain to analyze what was happening to me.

There wasn't even a hot chick around for my biological system to malfunction in this manner, apart from Jasmeet who had just passed without noticing us. I tried to swallow the big lump in my throat; but it didn't budge.

"Are you all right Dev?" Sid asked looking a bit concerned.

"Ah nothing, just gas I guess," I lied to him, and both of us burst out laughing.

"Yes, we just loaded ourselves with a lot of food right now!" Sid agreed.

It was a new phase in my life. Until then I was unable to find any soul who met my meaning of a friend. That's why when I met Sid, life suddenly became exciting.

It's a fact that when you start your college life you are known by the company you keep. Your group is the only way you prove your existence. Look at students from any college in any city; have you seen them hanging out alone? The two of us also wanted to make a steady group, not with infinite companions but with a few countable ones.

The pleasure always lies in togetherness. The plan was ready and from tomorrow 'Operation – *Dosti*' was going to start. While others started mingling with the hot chicks, spending lavishly on them in an attempt to fulfill the void of a beloved in their life; we two had a different opinion. Those hot babes, we thought, might spoil our relationship with each other and are hence not worthwhile to be with.

After having a quick scan of the bunch out there, we invited Ritesh, Jasmeet and of course Sheena as capable mates to pass the test under operation *Dosti.*

Ritesh was good at studies. After looking at his results (92%), one could only be convinced about what a genius he was, and after all there had to be someone to provide us with notes in the group! Teachers liked him but he was not any teacher's pet. He liked to wake up at exactly 7:00 am every day with his coffee, bitter with a single lump of sugar. His clothes were arranged neatly in rows, organized according to color. He was a man of principles; even his shoes were placed side by side, always at the same spot beneath his sock drawer, desk clean and free of clutter, with the pen-holder always placed on the upper right corner.

He liked everything to be arranged in the exact same way he wanted them to be. You see, Ritesh was the kind of person who liked his life to be filled with constancy.

He operated on the belief that if everything in life was in its place, constant and reliable, then life would be easier to handle. After all, people overcome their problems by sorting them out, surely if the little things were sorted out already, then there's more time for those bigger problems and thus, life would be easier.

And indeed, the principle worked quite well for him. His room was besides mine; so frequent interaction was a possibility.

Sid turned out to be an introvert in front of girls and would shy away; but Ritesh was just too perfect. Sheena loved our company with the chatter-box me and a hushed up Sid; but Jasmeet's face always exhibited a weird expression. Sometimes, she seemed to me as an actress in the movie 'Twilight' who could turn into a vampire the next second. I got goose bumps thinking about what it would be like to find her in my room, my bed, drinking my blood, sinking her teeth deep into my neck one night! I shivered at that thought. Mostly it was my fault; may be because I was all time so annoying to her, but then why did people like her have to get annoyed so quickly? It was difficult to match the frequency of my thoughts with hers, but still she was in our group.

"I hate you, you ass hole! You can go die for all that I care!"

"Yeah, well you aren't on the top of my list either, you lazy bitch!"

"Bitch? You are a self centered, manipulative, man-slut!"

"Hah! That hardly matches your caliber, does it?"

"Teri maa ki... Saala angrez... teri toh!"

I attacked her with various other verbal daggers having the highest degree of sharpness.

"*Bhaad mein ja*!" I stomped away. This was the third time that we had fought until we were satisfied and had screamed our lungs out at each other. But this time, the fault wasn't mine. Jasmeet's laziness and the unreachable book were to be blamed solely.

"Pass me the book," she said.

"Get it yourself," I said.

"Please pass me the book."

"Please get it yourself."

"Why can't you pass my book? It's right beside you!"

"Why can't you get the book yourself?"

"Why can't you be nice and just toss it over?"

"Why can't you shut up and get it yourself?"

"Why can't you pass it?"

"Why should I pass it?"

"Why shouldn't you pass it?"

"Why would I pass it?"

"Why wouldn't you pass it?"

"Why do you want me to pass it?"

"Why won't you pass it?"

"Why not stop being lazy and get it yourself?"

"Why not you just toss it over?"

"Why do I have to?"

"Why are you the closest one? JUST TOSS IT OVER!!!"

"WHY NOT-"

"GOD DAMN IT!!! SHUT UP YOU BASTARD!!!" she shouted slapping me hard and then I said some things and then she said some things and it just became a huge brawl before we knew it. I can't remember what the other fights were about; I think we just like to boast about ourselves to each other at this point of time. The only reason we were together was because her best friend Sheena was close to me and we all were in the same group. I went to the bathroom to calm down, she always got me so agitated that I felt like punching something or someone, maybe even her, if the time comes.

I looked into the mirror and saw my cheek was red with five fingers of the fairer sex imprinted on them. I did not care about what people said, maybe because I was so pissed off at myself. The reason was simple - I disliked Jasmeet. I don't know why, but I came to that conclusion last night. Her egoistic attitude was unbearable. I detested this trait. She was downright ridiculous!

I sighed and I heard the door open.

"Bratha? Are you okay?" It was Sid.

"I'm fine." I gave him a smile as my reddened cheek stretched and hurt.

"I saw that whole thing between you and Jasmeet. This is the second time this week."

"Third."

"Are you serious?!"

"Yeah."

"Well you guys really need help. This isn't normal."

"We hate each other. What's so abnormal about that?"

"It's how much you hate each other and why you hate each other that matters. It's like you both go out of your way to make each other mad!"

"It is she who makes me so angry!"

"But I'm also on the verge of suspecting something else. I'm starting to think it's just a cover up."

"A cover up… for what?"

"You both have feelings for each other."

My heart beats raced. He shouldn't have spoken this. If he spoke about the same to Ritesh, I was doomed. Ritesh would tell Sheena who would surely share it with Jasmeet, who in turn will torture me about it till the day I die or kill myself. The horror intended me to shut Sid's mouth, wondering if the proverb of walls having ears was true.

"Hell! No! I would never like that whore. She likes every other guy of our college," I whispered.

"Except you," Sid uttered.

"Well yeah, she hates me. I am aware of the bitter truth!"

"No I think she likes you enough to respect you. And why did you say the word 'Bitter Truth'?"

"She doesn't respect me! By the way which boy will like some girl hating him huh? But did you hear what she said – 'BASTARD'?!"

He sighed. "Like I said it's all a cover up."

"Bro, I realize you have some issues to solve, but that doesn't mean...

She called me a man-slut! I cannot let her speak that sort of rubbish! Not at all!"

"Dev you're only doing what she wants. Her goal is to make you angry and look at you now. You're furious, and she's out there saturated."

"Leave it Sid! I am not into these love melodramas. I am nineteen and I have never had a girlfriend. You might be thinking 'It is sad, huh?' but honestly I don't care. I don't like being vulnerable to such bullshit and making them think they are God's gift to men. I have always had this attitude because I don't want to fall head over heels for a girl and then get heartbroken."

"Gosh! Brother, you are such a wimp," he said as we parted ways. What I had said had been unacceptable for him, but the matter of fact was that I hated the love factor in life, and hence hated falling in love. I could like a girl but to love a girl was a big no-no.

Days passed like the wind and I consciously distanced myself from Jasmeet. The suffocation amplified as our brawls increased gradually and she got isolated. And just when classes started becoming a routine and the boring life set in, all of a sudden something happened; a debate competition was announced where we were supposed to comment on the topic -

'Modernization – a curse or a boon?'

One of our group members had to participate to keep our 'image' intact; but nobody had the guts. I thought to save and moved ahead. While others involved themselves debating and discussing the various pros and cons of the topic, I moved straight in front gathering every dumb head's attention.

"Guys I am done with my presentation, no need to bother."

They thought I was joking but then the thought turned in my favor when I actually began to speak. I was going to speak against the topic as if it was really a curse.

"Good afternoon, one and all present here. The topic for today is modernization and what it means in the 21st century.

It's a modernized culture we are living in.

The topic given doesn't relate only to the modern technologies; it also looks at a broader perspective which involves various fields such as science, technology, culture, values, perspectives, standards, etc.

Today we are equipped with posh houses to live in; electricity, cell phones, cars, air conditioners at our mercy and we call ourselves modernized. The technology factor has developed so rapidly that in a few years we will find surrogates all over to work for us.

It's true that these things are materialistic and they give us pleasure in life. They are machines, which serve their purpose at different points of time.

But...but...but! I have one question in my mind. Are you satisfied or do you want more reformation?

The economy is getting faster, every day we are becoming more modernized, the children are getting smarter and the education levels have increased. Our culture is getting broader and every individual has a right to live free and in peace. That was the positive side of the story; but have you ever tried to look at what we have lost in the meanwhile?

Finally, when we have achieved all this, can we be true to our hearts and say that we have achieved the real pleasures of life?

While we are in a race to succeed, we have left a lot of things behind which consist of human emotions, values and cultural factors. I will mention several points which will clear my stand.

Money today has lost its value.

The inflation rates have gone high. To comfort ourselves we earn more and more. The greed is taking control over us day by day. Selfishness has evolved inside each human and a thief has taken birth in each of our manipulative minds. A common man needs higher profits to fulfill his materialistic needs. He cheats and plays politics to make his wealth grow.

Under this concept of modernization, the rich become richer and the poor are just born to die. Money is all that matters now. Pause for a moment to think about these flaws while taking a step towards modernization. With life becoming a race, inflation has increased to such an extent that it is difficult to survive.

Your earnings have to be a lot more than what is actually needed. Many plan to go abroad to earn, leaving their family and when they come back to enjoy their riches; their parents have already passed away.

The culture is going to the dogs.

Gadgets have become a part of life making us all 'techno-savvy'. We survive with a craze of 'whose phone is better than whose?' This blindness to come first in our rat races is going to lead us to a miserable end. People have become so lazy with the use of technology that the obesity levels among people is increasing day by day.

If you haven't saved enough it is going to be tough later on to survive. Do you realize that any goddamn gangster may blow your brains away using the same technology, which is acting like such a boon until then.

Sometimes I ask a question to myself,

Are arms and weapons meant for our safety or for the purpose of destruction?

Note down my words, in the coming years when we have actually lived in our so-called modernized culture, we will find more abortion centers than provisional stores.

The next generation would have actually lost their Indian values because they live in a 'modern' environment. Now I ask you, are you still interested to live in a modernized world?

After what you have heard, I bet, maybe not.

So why are you alive in the 21st century? Go and stab yourself!"

Dr. Astha burst out laughing listening to my speech.

"It was just a provoked mind's thoughts," I said.

The next day we all gathered for the debate competition. The stage was dimly lit and chairs were placed on it on which a lot of distinguished people were seated. I felt confident and was eager to voice my thoughts out. One by one everybody came and expressed their views. It was Tehzeeb's turn now.

I was sitting next to Sid and looked at him; he was staring at her as if she were an entity dropped down from the heavens above. He got completely lost in her words in favor of modernization. Among all, she presented the best argument I felt. The confidence showed her true caliber. Now it was my turn to speak. I stood up from my seat smiling looking at the crowd inside the auditorium. While I was about to move Sid murmured in my ears.

"Lose the debate."

My smile faltered a little as I turned towards the podium. I was a little shocked. In the auditorium, there was a lot of whispering and talking going on. People had always praised my energy levels and this time they expected something different from their 'Dev'; maybe because I was their hero whom people expected to do well.

"I am going to speak against the topic," I said and a loud clapping sound greeted my words urging me to begin. Amongst the seven, I was the only one who was against the concept of modernization.

But why wasn't I speaking? Was I nervous? Was I scared? I remained silent for a whole half a minute. People were looking at me and I didn't have the guts to look at them. Silence prevailed and it continued to numb my mind. Then Sheena and Ritesh stood up encouraging me, gesturing me to speak out. They were also confused as to why I wasn't speaking. I looked into Sid's eyes to search for the reason why he was making me do this. He simply shook his head giving me an indication of being silent.

I was becoming a joke at the podium standing as mute as a statue.

I was still looking at Sid waiting for his orders. I wished that he would support me for my win and ask me to speak; but he didn't and I couldn't for the world guess why he was against it.

A few moments later as I continued to stare at him, he moved his eyes towards Tehzeeb. Standing at the podium, I didn't understand as to what had made him do that but then I understood what my wicked soul mate had wanted. His confidence in me made my dreams bigger but on the other hand he couldn't see Tehzeeb losing in the debate. He was her well wisher and only I could fulfill his wish.

Just for a smile on her pretty face, he had signaled me to let Tehzeeb win. I left the podium feeling sorry for having come unprepared.

I lost many hearts that day but won that stupid lad's confidence in me. It was then I realized that in life if you are not a self centered person, you will always find a person for whom you can even risk your life. You could do anything to get him out of a problem or a situation in which you think he shouldn't be. For me, now Sid had become that special being.

I remained silent with all these thoughts running inside my head. It was now time to declare the results and it was undoubtedly Tehzeeb who won the first prize trophy. I was sitting downstairs when Sheena came charging at me with a fuming frame of mind. I thought she was going to beat me.

Somehow, I had to deceive her and deflect her anger.

"I suddenly got butterflies in my stomach. Remember? I asked you about them and you spread the word around?"

That silenced her anger for the time being.

But I was glad that I could fulfill my friend's wish and I hadn't disappointed him. While we were sitting in a group Tehzeeb came forward to talk to me. Sid turned alert with his puppy love approaching.

"Hey girl! How are you feeling? Of course honored, right? And yep congratulations," I said raising my hand to shake.

"Thank you Dev! But nothing would have worked out so well without your co-operation," she said. Her words surprised me.

"It was your whole hearted effort that made you win," I said, my face wearing a blank expression disguising the feeling of frustration that was bursting inside me.

"Actually, while you were presenting yesterday, I was just sitting back there. I heard your speech and it was fantastic. If you had spoken, the trophy would be in your hands," she said making me feel like a helpless caught prisoner.

"I was stressed out, so couldn't articulate," I said.

"I don't think you were so tensed that you couldn't even utter a single word," Tehzeeb said gazing into my eyes.

For an instance, I was alarmed thinking if she had realized about Sid's lure. But then Sid was a shy jerk who would get all conscious and awkward if she got to know about him.

"There is an admirer, who wished that the wise should win. I didn't speak because he wanted to see you happy," I said.

"Oh my god! I'm so lucky. Who is he?" she asked me.

"He is someone dear to me and for his sake; may I have the honor of inviting you to my group?"

"I will think about your invitation and yeah, thank you for whatever you just did," she said while moving back towards her dorm.

"Don't give the credit to me because I didn't do anything for you," I said.

She stopped for a while and stepped back towards me, "Life gives a very few gifts in the form of caring friends. Your friend is the luckiest one to have you," she said and moved away.

The next day Tehzeeb poked her nose into our group's conversation without intimation. Sid's nervousness increased and his senses lost interest in everything around except her. She accepted my proposal to join the group. With Tehzeeb as a newcomer in our group, things started looking a little more happening. With a lot of whisperings that were exchanged around her, Tehzeeb finally got to know about Sid being her well-wisher. The other fact of the matter was still hidden – the secret love of Sid for his beloved Tehzeeb; and we did everything to get Tehzeeb close to him.

The more you try to hide something; the more the chances are for the cat to slip out of the bag. By not speaking it out, Sid's love for her became so strong that he now started being over protective about her. He never left campus and never went to his room without meeting her. Well, all had their own way of doing things. And something inside me felt good because both of them were getting mutually responsive.

Ah! The joy of watching hitching your friend!

3

It was the end of another ordinary day at IMS.

The foundations of the building shook as the students thundered out like caged beasts seeking freedom. The voices of the chatter boxers still reverberated in my ears. I swear I still do not know what collegians have so much to gossip about.

Sid's head had another story to tell. His mind was now a pot of confused thoughts which mingled with the happenings in his surroundings, leaving him a little alienated from everything around. If I could read his thoughts, I am sure I would have seen Tehzeeb's peaceful smile disturbed by the pandemonium around; Tehzeeb's voice fading into the chattering and bickering students' voices; Tehzeeb walking towards Sid with the thundering sound of footsteps made by the students escaping out of the clutches of the boring professors. That's what love had done to my best mate.

In order to escape this sudden burst of collective human enthusiasm, he took out his I-pod and plugged the earphones into his ears. That was the only means of escape he could think of. He turned up the volume to the maximum to drown the voices and replace them with his favorite song – *"Juda ho ke bhi.. tu mujme kahi baki hai.."* We sat aimlessly along the corridor and stared blankly at the mass of students passing by.

Sid needed to wait for the wave of students to vanish for some sinister reason of his own.

Suddenly he stood up, and unplugging the earphones, he stared in admiration at Tehzeeb. She apparently came out of nowhere and approached Sid. It was her he had been waiting for. She always had this care free smile, a friendly tone and attitude which endeared her to everyone who knew her. But, today she wasn't the same. She was perturbed.

"What happened," I asked. "You don't look well."

"Nothing." she said in a subdued voice. "It's just a small matter gnawing at my mind."

She looked a sorry sight. Her eyes were puffy and her lips; dry and pale. Something was different; she wasn't even smiling as always. Sid had never seen her bearing such a distant and sad expression. "What is it?" Sid inquired, "You know, you can tell me."

For us she was just a friend but for Sid she was more than that. He strongly believed that there couldn't be another person like her; not even close to her. He admired her in a weird kind of way; and her current expression bothered him.

"It's Professor Suresh. He is acting like such a jerk. He calls me twice, sometimes even thrice for some or the other work to his office; and he keeps staring at me, even during lectures. He is rapidly crossing his limits and my respect for him is diminishing with each passing day," she almost sobbed.

Anger flowed from Sid's aura as he heard these bitter words. "The bastard, how dare he!!!" the mad ass screamed and rushed to the fourth floor removing his belt. I rushed to prevent him from doing anything insane that might get him thrown out of college. He was damn furious at the professor's insolence. Anger filled every cell of his being; he impersonated a volcano eruption!

I caught hold of him but he was still furiously and inexorably rushing forward. He wanted to break free from us to have a fight with the Professor; but I did not allow him to do so. Soon Ritesh and Sheena came to my rescue. They brought ice cold water to cool him down. Tehzeeb too joined us. She looked frightened and horrified. Something unusual was happening with her and she wept for mysterious reasons. Was it the professor's freaky behavior or Sid's extra caring attitude? The girl who got Sid's attention was lucky in my opinion; but for Tehzeeb it was soon turning into a curse.

We all told Tehzeeb to be cautious and avoid going to Professor Suresh's cabin even if he summoned her. That day, we even planned to watch a movie in the evening for a change to get over this hullabaloo. R-world sounded like a wonderful destination. It is 25kms away from the suburbs, but that didn't bother us.

All is well where money dwells. That holds true anywhere and everywhere. We thought of hiring a car for our leisure trip. Somehow Sid and I managed to arrange a Santro Zing from Shakeel *bhai* thrusting our monthly incomes into the poor man's hand. Shakeel *bhai* was a garage owner close to our college.

Sid and I fought for almost half an hour for the honor of having the driver's seat. Everyone thought it wise for me to drive looking at Sid's present condition. So I was driving with a promise to offer the steering to Sid on the return journey.

Trying to stay calm and collected, Sid hummed along with the song playing on the radio. It was a hot day and the air conditioning in the car wasn't working properly; he could feel the beads of sweat emerging on his forehead.

Alas! The journey was short and we reached our destination.

The movie was great and refreshing. Somehow the thought of passing the steering bounced off my mind completely and it was I who was driving again. Sid was sitting beside me and Sheena, Ritesh and Tehzeeb fit themselves behind. Nobody could give Sid's memory a competition. He was very particular about words and promises. When he insisted on driving, it was totally my fault to spurn that mad ass frivolously and then Crassshhhh...! We all jolted forwards with the impact of the collision. For a moment nobody moved; everybody was reeling over the shock of had just happened.

Then Sheena exclaimed, "Oh no..."

"Are you ok?" I asked, concerned.

"What did you do to the car?" she yelled at Sid, horrified at the destruction of the vehicle.

"I don't give a damn! First it was Dev and now you. I am pissed off badly," he retorted.

"Um...He's going to fine us or call the police, I'm sure," Tehzeeb urged from behind.

"Thank God we are alive, that's the main concern," Ritesh said after getting out.

"Can anyone help us?" I shouted. A group of people quickly came forward to help. We got out safely. We were saved. Pushing the car aside and taking out the water bottles, we stared at each other and silently looked into the eyes of people around. I never thought that a plea would make so many people gather; but then, who doesn't like to see an accident?

The car, which was at the speed of a hundred and ten had reversed and collided with a loaded truck. Its headlights were gone and the bonnet was smashed. Miraculously, we managed to survive and get out of the wreck. I felt as if I was watching a movie with a brilliant gory twist in it!

I couldn't hear a thing over the pounding of my heart.

"What a horrible day!" I exclaimed.

After things got settled with the affected truck driver, it was time to move back to the hostel. This time Sid was driving the mangled car and I was sitting beside him fiddling with the radio to pass the time.

"Chill out," said Sid as he tried starting the car. The car sparked and barked, but absolutely refused to start.

"How the bloody hell do you expect us to chill out?" I shouted.

"Just breathe easy man, take it easy…in and out, in and out," Ritesh urged from behind demonstrating that Baba Ramdev's exercise. I looked at them simultaneously, shell-shocked; we almost got killed and they were asking me to chill?

"Do you two realize we almost got killed?" Sheena frowned supporting me, while Tehzeeb kept mum.

"Well yeah, but don't forget, my friends, the wise saying of the *Bhagwat Geeta*, that everything happens for the good," Sid said solemnly professing his thoughts.

"Oh… Really? How do you plan to fix this genius? We have less than 24 hours to return this car!" I screamed.

For the first time I saw Tehzeeb, quiet, shivering and trying to calm her frizzled nerves.

Finally the engine started and we went on our way; but halfway down the road it again began sputtering and gurgling, spewing oil.

Sid glanced at me.

"Uh… Now what?" I asked icily.

"Well, we're almost out of fuel and the car is about to stop," he whispered.

"I filled in a thousand bucks of fuel, how come it's over?" I shouted.

"The accident probably damaged the fuel pipe and caused it to leak," he professed pulling the car over to the side of the road. We all got out and looked for a sign that would point us in the direction of the nearest fuel station, but no luck there. We were in the middle of nowhere, without fuel or food. I pulled out my cell phone, and guess what, no network!

"Guys do any of you have a signal?" I asked hopefully. I didn't hear an affirmative response; oh yes, I wasn't a very happy man.

Ritesh was talking to some *Deh-Haatis* (they seemed like gypsies) who were walking along the road. I ran up to them and asked, "Do you know where the fuel station is?"

They looked at me confused, so I repeated myself. Then one began talking in a strange tongue, *"honnu… honnu…"* I looked at Ritesh who responded, "They don't speak English or Hindi you dumbass!"

It was almost nine and there wasn't a single soul apart from us on the highway. I did my regular prayer to God with an apology. "I'm the son of the creator of this cosmos, please help me out."

Pray from your mind and all your sins will come forward; but I prayed from my heart and gradually found God coming to me disguised as a truck driver. Finally we saw a ray of hope. We loaded ourselves along with the wrecked junk somehow and headed towards the hostel.

Dad was going to kill me if he got to know about the accident. We went to a nearby garage where the mechanic gave us an estimate of the damages caused. I didn't know that it would come up to twenty; I wish they would have meant hundreds.

While I was looking at the condition of the car, Sid went to talk to the manager.

"Ok fine, repair it as soon as possible," Sid spoke as if he had lacs inside his pocket. Sometimes I can't help myself balking at his overconfidence.

"What rubbish! Where will we get the money from?" I asked in a hushed voice.

"Don't worry! We'll do some setting," he whispered.

"You got any sources?" I exclaimed.

"No," he said giving me a strange look.

"Then any cash balance, savings or money in the bank?"

"No..." Sid muttered after a few seconds of ponder.

"Any friend who could give us a loan?" I questioned.

"I don't think anybody will have such a huge amount," he said.

"Then how the fuck you will arrange for so much money?" I asked, enraged.

"Why do you keep asking me these dumb questions?" Sid continued making me angrier.

"I am not an idiot you know! Why are you so exasperatingly calm like you have a convenient solution chalked out for us when I am losing my head here thinking how we should be getting the money?" I bursted out. For some strange reason, my questions seemed to amuse him.

"What will I say to the owner?" I sighed with a worried face.

"Be positive." A thin-lipped smile crossed his pale face.

I was outright furious, and I vented out my anger with a Whammm! A punch that made contact with the calm Sid.

"Ouch! That hurts Dev," he said faking a serious expression as he put his hand on his chest. He then put on a poker face; that he was a player came as no surprise to me. All guys are like him, excluding me!

"You know you have no choice," I shouted again.

"Don't worry, we'll take the car in two days," he nodded goodbye, and slinging his bag over the shoulder, he walked out.

"I think we live in the same junkyard," I shouted from behind.

"Then whom you are waiting for? Join me," he said. Times like these made me wonder if I really knew my friend or not, that crazy bastard he was. In times like these he seemed so deep and all knowing; but somehow he wanted to escape from my questions.

"You—you have made a mistake," I stammered.

"How are we supposed to get out of this? If you think I can arrange the amount, you are mistaken. I have the last 50-rupee note in my wallet. Monthly installments from Dad are due for a later date and if you are planning to take that away, I'm sorry I will not sacrifice it."

"Don't irritate *yaar*; I said *na*, I will do something."

The girls overheard our conversation and gradually came out with a solution, offering 15,000 bucks collectively. It would be a matter of shame not only for Sid but for me too, if we dared to accept those pink papers.

We left the car and the matter there itself, moving out of the service station to our den in an auto.

"How much *Bhaiya*?" I asked for the fair.

"Fifty," said the Auto*wala* and my dream of spending the last fifty on the junk demolished. Shakeel *bhai* got all our installments coming from our home sweet homes, leaving us penniless.

The pressure increased in the coming days. On one hand we had exams dancing over our heads, while on the other we were awaiting the figure (bill amount) which we were going to receive as a gift from the service station. Somehow it was easy to make *Shakeel bhai* understand the story but the deadlines to pay the gigantic amount seemed monstrous. I felt doomed…

Two days later, there was a call from the service station asking us to take away the car on making a payment of Rs.21, 556=00. I asked Sid about the arrangement but he was still blank. We couldn't go to our parents and nobody was ready to trust us for a loan. All options were blocked.

I wondered for a long time letting my thoughts float in the air that blew past the balcony of my hostel room, frightened, mumbling to Shakeel *Bhai* for one last chance to repay.

"I have something to sell," I told the sales manager.

It took me every inch of determination I possessed, to not turn around and walk out of the door, pretending to have walked in by mistake. The only thing that kept me steady was the fact that I was not the first person to stand in front of a jeweler's shop holding the only item I never thought I will part with; my precious gold chain.

"Am I supposed to guess what it is?" he asked sarcastically.

"Oh!" I pulled the gold chain out of my jeans pocket. It contained a pendent which fell on the glass counter.

"Its twenty-two carat gold," I proudly said. "My father gave it to me on my birthday."

My neck felt shivery and naked without the chain.

"I will give you nine," he said blankly.

"Thousand…?" I urged.

"No, hundred. What do you think?"

"It's worth at least 10 times that!" I retorted.

"I am not the one who needs the money," the owner reminded me conveniently.

"It's not gold but a replica, which means gold-plated."

I took off placing the darn chain inside my jeans pocket, cursing my dad all the way back for giving me fake gifts. I was completely screwed up from all sides.

I started to think of myself as an ordinary person who continued to have extraordinary experiences.

"Are you coming to the class?" Tehzeeb inquired, looking at our dull faces. "No mood *yaar*, you carry on," I replied sullenly. She stood there silently for a second hoping that I would have a change of mind and say the magical word, 'Yes'. Tehzeeb wanted to know the reason behind our sad faces; so stupid of her to have not guessed.

So I answered her with all my sarcasm pumped into an improbable story. "Actually my buffalo at home died today. She was kept with a farmer who used to provide us milk every day. Now that she has died, I am very sad. The buffalo was dear to me;

my lovely buffalo. My mom made *kheer* from her healthy toned milk every Tuesday."

Sid added, "That thing made up of rice, milk, almonds, cardamom... mmm… hmmmm…"

"I will not get that taste anymore. My sadness reminded Sid of *kheer* too. Now he wants that delicious sweet but we have no source for *kheer*; so even he is sad."

"Oh! What a sad story!" She reacted with surprise. Then a knowing smile crossed her lips. "Don't worry! I will write notes for you guys, on whatever will be taught," Tehzeeb said.

"Heee... that would be so sweet of you," I grinned sheepishly and we parted from her.

"So… where do you want to sit and repent so we can receive some more condolences?" I asked Sid.

"I am thinking of the same thing, coz that shouldn't demand money at all," Sid muttered.

"Shall we go to Barista?" I said in excitement.

"300 rupees."

"Hmmm...How about bowling or a movie then?"

"Minimum 150 bucks."

"Let's have a cup of tea. That's in our budget."

"20 rupees," he said.

"Why twenty? Since when did tea get so costly?" I asked doing some mathematical calculations.

"No the *muska* bun which you will gulp down along with the tea is costly. I know fatso, you can't resist it," he elaborated with a smile.

And so the elaborate planning process on how to kill time started. We sat idle for two hours without any junk food or cola, thinking about the solution to our many problems.

During break time at the mess, Sheena demanded, "Why weren't you guys in class?"

"Actually my buffalo died this morning…" and Tehzeeb couldn't stop her laughter on hearing my lame joke again.

Narrating my joke for the second time still seemed funny to me, but Sid was still worried about the car expenses. While we departed to the service station to get a solution, the girls along with Ritesh carried on with their daily routine.

We reached our destination and found that the car was ready. For the first time in my life, a good repaired car was giving me such a feeling of foreboding. 'What next?' it seemed to ask me. In some other situation on some other day, I would have been all excited to drive and test the four wheeled darling. There has always been this intense connection between men and their automobiles, and I was no exception to this.

The manager asked us to pay the bill. I counted the bill amount for the second time, just in case the bill had miraculously doubled; but math is math and two plus twossss, unfortunately, did not sum up to 7; the total came up to the same.

I took the manager into confidence and told him the whole story; but it seemed like shouting on deaf years. What could the manager probably do? After all he was just an employee. He gave us seven more days to pay the bill amount. Till then, the car was in his custody. Shakeel *bhai* too, had given us the same deadline to return the car.

One more day, ended and we had nothing to offer as a solution. Sleepless nights awaited us. The body did not adjust to the change in routine making us feel tired and listless during daytime; thinking about the only thing which was eating us, inside out.

The exam pressure was gnawing at me too. Each and every time I managed to catch hold of a book, I found myself paying lesser and lesser attention in its contents. We neither went to college, nor had any interaction with anybody.

But then frustration didn't leave us alone even as we locked ourselves up inside our messy room.

That day we turned up on campus to see our group at five. It wasn't for me but for Sid. It had been more than a day since he had called Tehzeeb or met her. He would meet her daily a hundred times under normal circumstances; but now he had his own limitations. Still he could hear her playful voice in his head as if she was there. I don't know why he opted to meet her rather than miss her; but I had by now learnt to not reason out with the working of

Sid's swinging mind. This time it was my problem and yes, his problem too.

We waited for her to arrive. She came out of college almost crying. Her nose was red; eyes all watery. Tehzeeb was about to cry but 'why?'

It was the question only she could answer.

The only thing that held her tears back was that she hated making a scene of herself in public. She walked towards Sid; he forgot all my problems after he saw her like that. Nothing was more important to him at that point of time; not even his own problem. He loved her more than anything else in his life. She was his lady love after all.

"It's Professor Suresh," she said, and then let out a loud cry. Her tears said something. Maybe she was hurt but what had happened could probably be disclosed only after Tehzeeb settled down.

"But what happened?" I exclaimed.

"He thought I was cheap enough to comply with him if he handed me the Management exam's question paper." She sobbed as she crumpled the question paper which got stuck in her *duppata*.

Did he cross his limits again?" Sid asked.

"He tried, but my slap stopped him from his deeds and then I came running all the way down to you all," she replied.

"I told you not to go to his cabin, then why did you do so?" Sid exclaimed on top of his voice accelerating from a low to high pitch in a matter of a second.

"He called me in the middle of a lecture for an assignment; what could I have done?" she cried.

"That asshole…" muttered Sid and started striding towards the professor's cabin. I had to stop Sid as soon as possible, before he turned the whole issue into something infinitely worse.

"I need to see Professor Suresh urgently," Sid ordered the peon.

"He left quite early to go home, anything critical?" he enquired.

"Mrs. Suresh had just arrived on the campus to see her husband," I said.

"I think she is pregnant," Sid whispered into the peon's ears.

"At this age, it's quite strange," he said being surprised.

"Might be a mistake but we deserve sweets tomorrow from the professor. She is standing downstairs; we need to talk to him urgently."

"Note down his number – 9824546053."

"What will you do with this number man?" I asked Sid while he was searching for something inside his wallet. "Do you have some change?" he asked.

"We need to beg even for this," I giggled. Finally he got a coin to dial.

"Saab! Behenji bole sabzi leke aana, kidhar leke aana woh nahi bole"

"Mera number aapko kisne diya?" asked the irate professor.

"Saab hum aate baki sab baat batate, pehle bolo kidhar aana"

"B-5, Manali towers, Drive-in," he said and hung up the phone. Sid was really mad, I could understand now. What a mind he had to have devised a plan under such anger! His plans were always weird and I strongly felt that if I took part in them, a visit to the jail wasn't far away. But somehow if I didn't stop him or be with him, I was sure he was going to wreak havoc on the door step of 'B-5, Manali towers.'

On reaching the door, "Suresh...*kidhar hai?"* Sid asked rudely. His voice was like a *mawwali,* a loafer, as if he was Shakeel *bhai's* punter.

"What?" his wife snapped as she opened the door.

"Ohh! Sorry for his words," I apologized.

She hesitated, then stepped back to let us enter. "We were looking for Professor Suresh to solve some doubts. Can you call him if he is here?" I asked in a sophisticated tone to Mrs. Suresh.

"He just left 5 minutes ago for some work," she replied as politely as she could manage, in complete contrast to Sid, who was fuming like a volcano.

"Tell your husband to stop being a jerk and at least spare girls his daughter's age," Sid threatened Mrs. Suresh who I thought was frightened enough at the sudden outburst, to not utter a word in front of us.

I elucidated the entire story behind Sid's unethical attitude before leaving her place. She boiled in anger too listening to what had been happening behind her back, giving Sid some momentary satisfaction; but the wrath inside Sid still kept him fuming.

Just as we were leaving the building, a brand new Honda CR-V painted in black caught our eye. "Who owns this chick?" Sid asked the security guard.

"Woh apne panch number mein Sureshji hai na," he replied nonchalantly and that little smile turned to a wicked grin within seconds; I realized what mischievous thoughts his brain had begun cooking. "No… no way, Sid you are not going to do that," I begged.

"*Professor ho ya uski gaddi, kee farak padta hai?*" he said, smashing the headlamps with a hockey stick.

"Stop yaar! Have you gone mad? Oh shit! Headlights gone?" I yelled as I saw the security guards noticing us and our antics from a distance. They were a little shocked at this sudden reaction of Sid. I wondered what their next step would be; call the police or stop him personally.

"Now seriously, why are you hitting the car?" I tried reasoning but in vain. A sickening smash of wood over metal and the bonnet broke; then the windshield cracked.

"Now that's quite a heavy price to pay for trying to act cheap with a girl. When he realizes the damages that he has to pay for; it would be the most expensive experience of the professor's life," I grimaced looking at the scenic beauty that Sid's rage had created. "All of this will cost him at least ninety thousand bucks," I exclaimed.

"Ours is just twenty one," Sid answered. We stood face to face with our ironical fate, gazing at the car that we had just damaged.

All I needed was a handkerchief to wipe off the sweat flowing down my face. I got my hands inside those deep cargo pockets but nothing other than a piece of paper could be found. I used that, crumpling it into a ball for a shot. It took a few seconds of silence to realize that what I had wiped my face with was actually a million dollar baby to us.

I rushed to the paper and my happiness knew no bounds when I found that it was the day after tomorrow's Management exam question paper which Tehzeeb had given me.

I tried to read the serious expression on Sid's face. I thought if he had the same stupid thought.

"So…are you in? By distributing the paper we can fuck Suresh's ass more tightly. He has dug his own grave, after all," I elucidated.

"Yes," Sid nodded in agreement. "First his wife will screw him up, then the fucked up car and finally the leaked paper. Even his father won't understand who the fuck was behind the professor's grand screw up story," he giggled.

'Gentlemen, all ears here! This is your supporter Dev with a special offer tonight. For the first time in the history of IMS, somebody has identified the loops hole and managed to get the exact question paper for the day after tomorrow's Management exam. You are one of the four bidders who could respond to me with an amount. The highest bidder wins!'

Above was the message sent to four prospective clients as an open invitation to our offer?

Now we got this opportunity to start our new business venture wherein lads of rich daddies were invited to bid for the paper. The bids came through messages and we got two genies who agreed to pay us 15000 bucks each for the paper.

'Deal' was the final word we shared with our first client. It's a rule of every business to provide fringe benefits for utmost customer satisfaction. Sid was a master in this field. He got all the answers ready with illustrations to make this deal fruitful, the next time too.

Payment terms were somewhat like fifty-fifty before and after exam. Though it was a risk if somebody else got to know the story; we took assurance from them to keep mum.

It's rightly said, "When you cannot keep your secrets, don't expect others to keep them for you."

One of our clients stole the business idea and became a king without our knowledge. He too messaged prospective clients for bids and in return recovered almost 160 percent of his investment from two more guys.

This chain continued and we became aware of it when the forth guy personally messaged me to bid for the same paper. We kept mum deciding that the paper was history for us.

The only thing which kept us steady was the fact that we guys weren't the only nerds who leaked the paper. The next day after the paper, everybody came outside smiling, bragging over the fact of how wisely they had managed to get the exact question paper.

We got our payment which in turn was used to pay the service station bill; all thanks to Tehzeeb. After the exam, Sid had to go out for some work.

As he was moving out, he took my phone to use in case of urgency. We all were enjoying our usual 5 pm gossips.

Everything was special at that point of time. Our group felt like the most heavenly place to be on the face of this earth. Some people give funky names to their groups, some wear similar t-shirts for gaining attention; but none of us opted for any of those.

We were a simple group happy amongst ourselves.

When we came together as a group for the first time, it was 5pm in the evening. It was a great day. We did lots of chick-chatting rather than talking about each other. At the end when everyone was departing, it was Sid who wished to make this moment memorable. He saw the time which showed an exact five pm.

The evenings turned out to be the most wonderful part of the day for us from then on. It was a promise we made to each other; no matter what situation we are stuck in, till we are in this college, we will meet each other every day, same place, same time. We will never miss this five pm moment for the duration that we are in college. Who knows? After college we may sit someday sipping a lonely coffee in our homes thinking of our 5pm chats and smile to ourselves. From that day hence, this event became a part of our daily lives.

"Hey buddy! I'm back," Sid burst out from behind me with a box in his hand. It was wrapped. I strongly felt that it was for Tehzeeb and a sudden pang of jealousy hit me which made it a little difficult to ask about it. Ah! The prick that one feels when his best mate's attention is divided!

"Is there something special in this box?" I managed to ask.

"Yes indeed there is, for my brother Dev," Sid announced as I felt my jaw drop.

"Are you serious?" I jumped with excitement.

"The only other time that I have received a gift was when my father gave me that fake gold chain on my 18th birthday. After that, my eyes have always starved to see a gift wrapped for my hands to open," I said with all my heart as I opened the wrapped box.

As soon as I opened, there was no limit of my happiness.

"Are you crazy?" I hugged Sid with joy.

It was the new Nokia N-gage silver black phone.

That was the happiest moment of my life. Yes, he was passionate in almost everything, this guy; and friendship was no exception.

"Where is the older one?" I asked.

"That was old and wrecked enough, so I sold that off and bought the new one paying the difference from our joint balance." My excitement levels got higher when I discovered that he had spent all our money which we had made from our new business venture.

"Can't you keep that money for one day in your pocket?" I said scolding him mockingly, for the unnecessary expense.

"Don't nag me like a housewife. Besides, it's better to spend the black money as soon as possible before people start making claims for it."

"How may that be possible? We gave the exact paper and our job is done."

"There are some questions you should leave for the future to be answered," He said and took the phone from my hand.

Whatever it was, I had got my favorite phone. Sid's memory was sharp; very sharp to have remembered my words that the N-gage silver black was in my wish list.

The next day our cell phones didn't leave us alone for a second; the calls were not letting us study. The lads of the rich daddies had never thought that the previous offer would result into such a bonanza for them. They seemed to have turned entrepreneurs overnight. They had got the question paper for peanuts and made lump sum profits gaining the customers' trust at one shot. The chain of phone calls had started from the end users and had finally reached us. Our clients waited with the expectation that we will get another exam paper for them. The demand was high and this time we could get higher prices for the paper.

When Sid thought of leaving the matter, I had some other stupid plans. I took the textbook and made a dummy paper for the spoilt brats. This time we messaged thirty small sharks instead of ten dolphins or four blue whales about the new paper scheme. Pirated stuff is always defective and hence we took no guarantee of the authenticity of the paper. The offer was simple; the interested may pay and avail, the rest may leave.

We arranged it in a format just like an exam paper and got 30 copies to sell. Because of many free holders, we didn't earn as much as expected. This expectation wasn't mine but Sid's who had already planned to earn as much as 0.3 million from our joint business venture.

It seemed ironical when the pirated version got sold at a prize higher than the original one that we had sold previously. It appeared that luck was on our side or we were on luck's side, but someone or something was going to fuck after the luck failed to serve its purpose. It was difficult to manage the balance we had started getting. Day after day, with each exam we made good profits except for the last one.

The paper was all set and like every scheme, we got this one out. Our balance was racing towards Sid's expectation. The next day came as quite a shock; out of 20, only two questions came from the paper distributed. Like all exams, everybody had so much faith in us that they didn't read anything beyond what we had provided.

We both finished the paper early and ran before the public got violent to beat us up after the exam.

We disappeared like a pie from the clutches of a ravenous fatso.

"Oh yeh… oh yes… oh yess"

"Tell her to mute Dev, she's so loud!" Sid banged the bathroom door of the IBIS hotel, Pattaya, where I was fulfilling the wonderful purpose of life for which God has sent us on earth. A joy ride of an hour was more than enough.

"*Khapan-ka,*" the Thai call girl greeted Sid as she came out of the bathroom.

"*Ma ke lo...*" Sid's face was worth looking at. He was some kind of a *brahmachari* who kept his virginity for his lady love. Gifting virginity? That didn't sound like a great idea to me. Sometimes I got bouts when I felt like 'what the fuck, why the fuck am I fucking people'; that's when I respected Sid the most; Sid with his ethics, principles and virginity-dignity proverbs.

He had just one vice; smoking. That was all he did to divert his mind from the girl who was caught inside; I write 'caught' because of his over possessiveness for her. Though 75 percent of the chicks at college longed for Sid; it was he who couldn't and wouldn't go beyond the girl of his dreams.

She seemed to be with him 24/7 like a shadow moving with him, staying with him. While he was with me in the amorous hell on earth a.k.a. Pattaya's walking street, his mind stayed in heaven i.e. our college for the only girl he detested and truly loved– Tehzeeb, who else? The sound of her laughter, her smiles and her actions drove Sid mad. He could not digest the fact that there was a person like her existing in this world who had made such an impact on him. Every time he didn't see her presence, it annoyed him. I think he enjoyed the essence of her radiant company; which he preserved like a priced possession.

After almost two weeks of enjoyment and joy, we thought of packing our bags and leaving for Sid's heaven; our college. The final exams had been adventurous but the next semester seemed to be quite the opposite. Our group thought of using the vacation period wisely instead of spending lazy and idle days at home. The proposal submitted to the management was fantastic and every student at IMS had to bear the consequences. College started early with new projects on the charts. When we reached our hostel room after our vacation, it looked like a junkyard as we tried maneuvering ourselves in the sea of unwashed clothes lying all over. I opened the window for some fresh air. It was good to be back in the one place where I could truly relax and breathe the fresh morning air.

Brut totototoot....puk!

"Oh, shit! Come on Sid! Do you have to do that here, you shitty bastard!" I had covered my nose instantly so couldn't smell his fucking fart; but it was to strong that I almost tasted it.

Vacation was over and a new semester had just started with the declaration of results on a first hand basis. Tension prevailed among all the students of IMS. But here what occupied my attention was the reason that was causing such horror. They weren't tensed for their results; it was the notice displayed on the soft board outside class that was making everyone uneasy. This notice stated,

Hello students,

Something strange has been going on among the first

year students and I feel sorry to declare that only 12 students out of ninety have passed in the first semester's exam. A strange reaction has been expressed by our professors who seemed to be confused on how this can happen. The list of failures also includes those students from whom we had great expectations.

To get to the bottom of this disaster and to investigate further, a team of professors will surely turn up to your class to discuss the matter. Till then no single lecture will be conducted for this semester.

Rajpal Sinha

(Chair person)

The notice spread like a virus among the students. Everybody was waiting for things to appear as straight and clear as possible. The next lecture seemed like a judgment day. Rumors travelled across the campus making a chill run down the spines of our dishonest customers who leaked the paper without our knowledge.

"Good afternoon students," the chair person greeted us as he walked into the classroom. "For the first time in the history of this institute, something unusual has happened. I have never encountered such an event. Not one, two or four; but almost every student has been proved guilty by the professors."

"Look at this answer sheet," the Dean continued planning to read out loud from an answer sheet. "This answer sheet belongs to Vivek Singhal, Roll no. 89."

"On a particular question about, 'Is management, an art or a science?' our fellow student has explained it superbly. Vivek explains that, 'Management is both art and science. It is the art of making people more effective and productive than they would have been, without you intervening. The science lies in how you do that. There are four basic pillars of management: plan, organize, direct and monitor.' The perfection behind this answer is elaborated with a mind blowing example he has given below.

The example states that Mr. Adam is a bachelor who wants his son to be a student of St. Lawrence School for nursery in the September 2011 batch exactly seven years from now. Let us see how management plays an important role for Adam.

1. Our dear friend Adam starts looking for a bride in the year 2003.
2. In the year 2004, he gets married to Chitralekha, ruining his wonderful bachelor's life.
3. Years 2005 and 2006 bring with them a lot of wonderful memories in terms of promotion and a blissful married life.
4. If September 2011 is what dwells in his mind; he would only be obliged to receive a child if his wife conceives in August 2007. But what if he fails and the process gets delayed? In such

situations, planning and monitoring plays an essential role. Mr. Adam has already kept a three month buffer period to get his desires fulfilled on time. One thing to be noted is that 'Management is not applicable and hence not responsible for consequences under unnatural circumstances.'

5. As directed by his own instinct Mr. Adam plays the role of an individual performing the art of management. In simple words it can be said that to get information about a subject is science and putting that information to practice is an art.
6. With apt implications of both science and art, August 2008 bring happy winds to our dear Adam's life when a baby boy is born in his family.
7. And finally, after 3 years his son gets admission into the school of Adam's choice.

In conclusion management can be described both as a science nd as an art. As a science it directed Adam (through his principles) to use their practical efficiency and as an art, management gave the strength to face any situation."

The professor stopped suddenly and took a close look at everybody. My reaction to him was surprising as I gave a standing ovation with a loud clap for the example. Even Sid joined me; but it was only Sid who had joined me in the entire class. Everybody else had faces with guilty expressions as if their parents had seen them masturbating. It was then that the professor picked another answer sheet and started speaking solemnly.

"This answer sheet belongs to Vikas Bhatti, Roll no. 90. In the same question about, 'Is management an art or a science?' our fellow student has written the very famous definition from Kotler like our genius Vivek did; but here too the name of the protagonist and the illustration seems Xerox copied. For an instance I was angry why these two students cheated but to my surprise the chain got longer and continued to students sitting a floor above them to write their examinations."

"Didn't get my word?" The professor spoke, trying to be as polite as he could; failing to keep the icy sarcasm out of his voice.

"Prachi Desai, Roll no. 3, got a new definition for the same question but why the hell is fucking Adams wife pregnant here too? It's not this example which bothered me but the fact that 78 students got the same Adam fucking his wife in October 2008, for his child's admission. I would have spared students for similar writing but only if it was a single question or a single exam paper. Economics got 62 similar answer sheets, Business organization 45 and English literature 70, principles of Management topping the charts with a 78."

"I wonder how people couldn't make it in Business Math? Forty students failed because their answer sheets were blank."

"I need an explanation immediately," the chair person roared at the top of his voice, venting out all his pent up anger.

The situation was getting worse and we could do nothing except panic. We couldn't fully trust the people who had bought the paper from us. Unity was still lacking and we were left to face the consequences. You cannot hide a cat for long in your bag; so before anybody got the opportunity to expose us, I stood up for an explanation.

I walked to the front of the room and stood there, hunched up like a scarecrow, with my eyes vacant, face blank, as if I was a criminal facing a trial. Minutes passed but I was unable to break silence. I looked at Sid waiting for the answers running through my mind to come out of my mouth. The only thing he did was wave a folded spiral document to & fro. I cursed myself for being so slow to understand what his eyes were saying me all this while. Sid was really a genie. I smiled and sat down. The professors were annoyed at this behavior of mine; but then I had a gift for them kept inside my bag. I took out my notes and offered them to the chair person. The front page said, 'LMR' by Sid Agrawal. It was then that I had the guts to speak the truth.

"Sir, I understand your uneasiness but if you see the other side of the same coin, you might change your mind. It's truly said that an institute is a knowledge temple for the students and the faculties hence directly translate as *Rishi muni*'s. We respect them, obey them and so they take the place of a *guru* in our lives. But let me bring some facts to your notice that will open your eyes to what is happening behind your back, only, if I have your permission."

The chair person was sure to give me permission after so much sophistication being showered on him. It was now time to go for the kill.

"1. Professor Suresh is a *tharkey*, a letch, who has been eyeing and attempting to abuse female students for some time now. Tehzeeb is one of the victims; I don't want to name others," and I suddenly changed the topic.

"2. Our English professor gave us the so called 'essential notes' on account of the incomplete syllabus and…

3. Sid Agrawal along with Ritesh took lectures by the night hours, performing the duty of our professors. This LMR document is a proof of his hard work, whose benefits every student sitting in this class has reaped and hence you can find its copy in every student's bag."

The over dose made the Dean look like a scare crow now when the students took out their Xeroxed answers as proof which we had distributed along with the paper. Professor Suresh had a bad day when his misdeeds were finally exposed publicly.

It was me, Sid and of course Tehzeeb, who had the last laugh that day. While Sid and me were jubilant about having got a clean chit; it was Tehzeeb who was ecstatic about getting the professor thrown out of the institute.

Our Dean, along with the students clapped for us, with different reasons on their minds; but Tehzeeb's appreciation awoke different feelings inside me.

She looked at me with all hopes and smiles as if I was her man and that she had waited for this day forever. Her emotions radiated like the sunshine inside the classroom. I felt as if everybody had turned blind and mute and it was only me feeling straight and complete. Her voice, her laughter turned so blissful with such a burst of emotions and happy vibes that I drifted away with them, crossing the border that I had never dared to step across till now.

It was that border of trust which Sid had in me.

4

I believe that there is absolutely nobody except a friend who can understand you inside out. Neither your parents nor your brother, nor anybody in this world can get into the position that a dear friend holds.

No matter how kind our parents are or how much love and luxuries they shower upon us, we are always going to long for something else. It's the need of a face which we want to see; yet we may not even know what it looks like. It is so ambiguous that we may not even recognize it, if it were before our very eyes.

Surrounded by the wonders of the materialistic world there is a raging void inside us; one which craves to be filled. Only a true friend can fill it because he personifies hope when our life seems to wander in the depths of despair.

When you meet a person, a girl or a boy, something clicks inside you and you start developing a hidden relation with them. A kind of relationship which evolves as an attraction and you become a little more affectionate towards that person. After some time, you realize that you simply cannot bear being apart. You become increasingly comfortable with their company that you have opted to keep. It's not implied because this feeling is quiet natural. This feeling, which develops deep inside you for the person you have just met, is none other than friendship. Day by day, the bonding gets so strong that you find only him as a trust worthy person in this world.

When you cannot keep your secrets to yourself and hence share it with the person whom you find more trustworthy than you yourself; he is a real friend for life. He is your true buddy and you end up giving him or her, a place above all relations. Once friendship reaches a level like that; no one can ever take the place of that special person, deep in your heart.

Sid walked into my life and in no time, we were instant buddies. The trust and the care, happened naturally between us; as if we were destined to be friends. But sometimes, circumstances are such that they may not let you go your way. It's a kind of an unreal quest that life places in front of you, and expects you to reach the end.

My life with Sid and Tehzeeb was going on smoothly. The second year of college was not only enthusiastic; but it was filled with a lot to learn. With projects and assignments on the charts and we trying to meet deadlines; everything seemed to be falling in place, but suddenly, something unusual happened.

4th August, 2004.

It was friendship's day. This day is amazing in every individual's life because it brings back memories of the past of how we had lived the good times with our closest pals. Human beings are social creatures and have always valued the importance of friends in their lives. Like every intense relation, friendship too is a multi-faceted relationship, comprising of a mixed-bag of emotions. Friends cry together, empathize with each other's agony, share happiness (& ice creams) and have a lot of fun together.

Sid's excitement was seen on his face. He needed a reason to show Tehzeeb how much he loved her and today he had got that opportunity. He would bring a broad smile on her face and wipe away all her tears with that teddy he had brought for her. His words always depicted how much he cared; but the care just got a small acknowledgement in terms of friendship. For Sid she was his world, but in her world Sid was just another nobody.

He wanted to be close to Tehzeeb and every thought made him move on the path that he had chosen for himself. Sometimes people fail against the will of God. This is where they feel low because things don't happen their way and as per their expectations.

It was a letter from Tehzeeb to me which became a matter of annoyance to him, me and everyone around.

To,

My sweet friend Dev,

This is my first letter to you and it took me all night to think, think and only think about how to start with, in the first place. I wish you a Happy Friendship's Day and I feel delighted to spend this special day with you. We are a special group. After a very long time, I am impressed and truly happy to find people like you. Our group is a huge support in life to me due to which I feel so relaxed and comfortable. It's good to learn new stuff and share things. I am glad that someone in this world has realized that sharing things only refines and grows oneself. All the credit goes to you for this wouldn't have happened if you hadn't invited me to your group.

My heart feels happy when I truthfully can say that by the grace of God, I made another special friend today. Till date you were just a companion who studied with me but today you stand for a different chapter in my life.

We cannot have too many for the courage that we need, if only in the comfort of a good and kindly deed. If only, in their counseling and the words of sympathy that leaves no doubt or question on their sincerity. And so it always is a day that has a happy end when I can tell myself that I have made another sweet friend.

Thanks for all the fun times and the sad times we've shared. Even though I have never known you completely, I feel that I have. So I am raising a toast with my glass of chilled coffee to you. Hope you have a special day today. Happy Friendship day once again!

With love… Tehzeeb!

The words were sweet but they could hurt somebody. I read it a hundred times wondering what feelings made her write such a letter. *Was it love? Was it friendship or was it something else?* I couldn't gauge the reason behind this, but one thing was sure; if Sid came to know about it, he would feel a stab in his heart. It was difficult from both sides. Either I hide the fact or I speak out what had just happened. Evil thoughts didn't leave my mind till I acted as a coward, hiding the fact.

My thoughts were the beginning of a tragic end. It's difficult to conceal a pie from a hungry man. Things became complicated when Sid found the letter inside one of my note books. He looked up at me, his chin trembling, and when I looked into his dark eyes, they frightened me. He stared at me as if he had never seen me before; as if I were a complete stranger to him.

That day he felt so bad, that he didn't speak to me for two whole days. I didn't have the nerve to tell him anything. Finally, I decided to speak to him. With a pounding heart, I confronted him.

"It was a small thing that you could have shared with me," he looked at me in amazement.

"I thought you wouldn't like it," I whispered with a murmur.

"Oh no!" Sid cried out, startling me. "Why did you make that wrong assumption? Why did you have to hide anything from me?"

I knew that he was feeling awful in his heart. That day I promised, I would never hide anything from him. "Shall I give her a card in return?" I asked.

"As you wish," he spoke with a creepy look.

"She is just a friend and a group associate. Don't get me wrong."

"And just in case you feel anything else, please tell me," he added with a straight face.

I just nodded and terminated the conversation there itself with my departure.

The next day Tehzeeb was surprised to receive a witty friendship card which I designed for her with colours and crayons.

"Thank you so much, Dev."

"No, don't be. I just gave this as a return gift," I said amusing her.

"Do you know something? You are brainless." She leered while opening the card.

It wasn't those quixotic types with hordes of philosophical expressions, but a simple one with humor inside.

I was waiting for that expression on her face to change, to know if she liked it. She just looked inside the card, then at me and burst out with an ear-splitting cackle. "Didn't you find anything else to write?" She said and then read out loud.

"Three male pencils and one female pencil were in a pencil box. If the female pencil got pregnant, who would be responsible for the crime?"

She paused for a moment, thinking; as if answering it was the jackpot question for KBC but then, "Will you tell me the answer?" she demanded, without applying any of her I.Q.

"The pencil without a rubber," I said and laughed as she joined me. It took minutes for us to settle down, but the next moment everything turned serious.

"May I ask you one thing?" I questioned moving a bit closer. I wondered if walls had ears, they would tell Sid about the thing that I was going to ask.

I huddled up closer to her. Her aroma was divine. I could feel her strawberry scent on me but then I focused my thoughts a 100% on the thing that I was going to ask her.

"Why did you give that card to me rather than to Sid? I mean, you could have given the both of us, if you wanted to. He is your best buddy and you know how much he cares for you. Isn't he your friend?"

"You have a flawed notion there. I consider him as a pal but that's it, with a big full stop. Do you know where the problem lies? He ponders a lot more over our 'so-called' companionship," she said.

"Why? Anything wrong in that? He likes you," I tried reasoning out with her.

"Dev, do you know why I wrote that letter?"

"Hmmm! You wanted to thank me now personally for the debate competition which I had left for you last year," I made an illogical guess.

"Aha... You are so wrong there. I am genuinely grateful for what you did, but the card wasn't for that."

"So what was it?" I asked her looking a bit tensed. She wasn't in a mood to joke. Her seriousness could easily be revealed through her words.

"I don't want Sid to get a wrong perception about me. I can be his friend but cannot stand beyond that for him."

"Is there an issue with him again?"

"There is always an issue with him; the problem is that it never ends."

"I think somebody has brainwashed you about Sid."

"Do you think that I am dumb enough to overlook the group politics going around? I know very well that Sid is attracted to me and day by day, he is getting obsessed with the Tehzeeb thing. And you people, instead of making him comprehend the drawbacks, are helping him with his obsession," she ranted.

"No it's nothing like that. You are on the wrong side of the whole thing. He likes you Tehzeeb and I think you should think about his proposal," I tried for Sid's sake.

"Every individual is free to choose his mate, I think," she seemed stubborn.

"So who is forcing you, friend? I just asked you to think about Sid."

"You don't tell me a thing! That is exactly what you people are doing now-a-days, and I'm so fucked up because of that. That day while we were sitting together, you went upstairs and called Sheena on her cell phone. What did you say? Prof Suresh was calling her and Ritesh on the 4th floor. What were you trying to achieve huh? Trying to give Sid some privacy with me?"

"No, actually Sir did call us," I tried proving my innocence..

"Oh! Come on, don't lie. That day if you remember Sir was not even present in college. We had a free lecture."

"Ah! Was that so?" I spoke in a soft tone, showing my dumbness.

"You are caught red-handed, any justifications for that?"

The questions were really tough to answer. But her expressions made me think about Sid and his possessiveness. When he was smartly planning things, Tehzeeb had been a bit extra smart and had come to know all; without any clues.

It was true that we were forcing that girl for Sid's desire. "I am sorry if I have hurt you. I didn't mean so. I just thought I should support my friend," I said sheepishly.

"I admire his inclination towards me but people around don't seem to take it in the right sense. My cousin, who is a junior here, has taken this gossip to his parents. Now just because I'm cool and collected, doesn't mean that I will stay quiet for a long time."

"I think you should give him a second thought before ending this relationship with him."

"First of all, there has been no 'relationship'; let me make that very clear to you. Everybody knows about us as a couple, thanks to people like you and it's a shame for me to be teased with a guy I don't have feelings for. That day also, when we were going for a movie, you punctured my Activa and forced me to go with Sid on his bike.

"I am sorry about that also, but how did you know?"

"Murli, the canteen guy told me."

I seemed to be ending up as a complete fool in her eyes. She turned out to be much smarter than my knowledge.

"One more time my parents bug me about the Sid affair and I'm out of the group."

Her one-liner was hammering in my mind. The practical part, which we did not even bother to look at, seemed quite painful and inconvenient to me now. She was understanding, caring, determined, kind and naive. But that was a facet of Tehzeeb she chose to show the world. I had seen her other '*Maa Kali roop*' today. She was so stubborn when angered. She had been incisive, brutal, careless and irrespective of me apologizing a million times; she would not let it go so easily.

Nevertheless, I knew how to convince her.

This time I honestly depicted the story. With the story, I shared my inner most feelings about Sid and our group. I got so comfortable that I realized I could speak anything to her without hesitation.

I promised her to make him understand that his attempts at achieving Tehzeeb's love were going to be fruitless. She was satisfied because now she had somebody to support her. While Sheena was supporting Sid without thinking of the side effects; I acted as *Narada muni*, taking both their sides from time to time.

The next day I forgot my cell phone in my jeans pocket. Tehzeeb called me as usual but I was out for some work. It buzzed twice before it came to Sid's notice. When the cell phone buzzed for the eighteenth time in just an hour; he thought he'd better answer the phone.

"Hey stupid where were you? I was so worried about you," Tehzeeb said.

"Sorry this is Sid here and Dev actually is out for some work. I will tell Dev that you were worried about him." He then disconnected the phone.

My arrival was going to bring havoc.

"What's going on?" Sid shouted as I entered the room. I had packets in my hand and he did not even give me a moment to put them down. I was scared knowing that the reason would surely be Tehzeeb; but I pretended asking what he was talking about.

"You know very well, Dev. Don't fool around. Tehzeeb called 18 times on your phone just because she was worried about you, do I look so stupid to not understand what is going on?" he questioned.

"Maybe, she had called for some personal work," I said.

"I have checked your log; does she have this personal work shit with you daily?"

"Dude! Are you spying? There is nothing like that between us. You are crossing your limits," I shouted.

"I don't mind if you chat but you didn't tell me about it," he shouted even louder.

"What is there to say man? We simply converse like normal friends do."

"Earlier you told me everything; then why are you hiding things today?"

"Well, I will remember your words buddy; now if I go to shit and not tell you, will you go around complaining again that I am not telling you things lately? What a baby you are, really!" I vented out a bit of my anger too.

I then turned a deaf ear to Sid's orchestra, which went on and on for God knows how long. I thought of letting things flow smoothly by only nodding and complying, paying no reasonable attention to Sid's words. I could now understand Tehzeeb's words about Sid's possessiveness suddenly. While I was taking all that a jealous mind could churn out; I couldn't figure out what Sid was trying to explain. Illusion plays a very bad role in our lives because what we see isn't real. Then we make our own perceptions about that illusion and fall a prey to uncalled-for sadness once the dream ends and reality strikes.

What I clearly understood was that Sid was mad; mad about the girl, Tehzeeb and that no one should ever mess with her and everybody better stay away. I remember what Dr. Astha had told, "It isn't your fault if she was comfortable with you."

I was surely going on the wrong track getting closer to the girl whom he cared for so much. I was taking her far away from him because as she enjoyed my company more and more, she started getting away from Sid and that was pricking him bad.

"It isn't as straight as it seems to be Doctor," I whispered.

Even I thought that if Tehzeeb was comfortable sharing beautiful words with me and not with him; it wasn't my fault. I was a human living life in a simpler way and that made her feel like talking to me. But this simple life of mine was hurting Sid so badly that he soon became a chain smoker.

Smoking is a silent killer. Sometimes it's all about putting on a show. We all think it's cool. But for Sid it was an addiction.

Every time he was late for class he had a lame excuse to give. We all knew it was the cigarette that made him come late; after having it twice or maybe thrice sometimes, he turned up to class. It all depended on his mood; one day he may smoke ten, the next day, maybe thirty. Cigarettes had become his fresh air and he needed his quick fix to enjoy his lifestyle, stress-free, skinny and cool.

I stopped him many times, but all in vain. How could I make him realize that he was being such a fool? His teeth started yellowing but he continued smoking like there was no tomorrow.

It was too late when I realized what Sid was trying to say that day. True friends never leave each other; even if one of them is walking on the wrong path in life. A true friend will try to correct the other in a way that it does not hurt the ego of the other friend. Friends don't mind when mistakes are pointed out; rather they try to accept it and change themselves for the better.

I shared everything with Sid and now with the advent of this girl I was acting like his foe in the name of friendship. The friendship that Sid and me had designed so beautifully, had reached a point where it would break into pieces with one false act of mine.

Everything settled down between Sid and me. The routine days were back again with the exam pressure riding high on our heads. This time we had no paper scheme and could hence concentrate more on our performances in the exam. A few days after the exams, I called Tehzeeb to meet up. I got my cell out as I headed out of the library.

I messaged Tehzeeb, "Meet me in an hour at the café."

I went to my room, changed, grabbed my bag and headed to the café. It was a huge place, deserted right now; but it looked beautiful when it was crowded with all the hustle-bustle of people animatedly talking and enjoying their conversations over steaming cups of coffee or cold sundaes.

I was standing outside waiting for my eyes to have a glimpse of her image. Suddenly someone grabbed me from behind. One hand covered my mouth preventing me from screaming while the other held my hands down so I couldn't escape.

"Who are you?" I asked.

"Bhoot!" Incredibly relieved I swung around, "Tehzeeb! You little idiot you almost gave me a stroke, why did you have to come sneaking up on me like that?"

I looked at her. She was beautiful in a unique way with chiseled features and long shiny hair. I would have loved running my fingers through that hair.

"Why did you call me here? Are you planning to take me out on a date?" she said grinning all alone at her lame joke.

"Be serious, I wanted to say something to you," I said.

"That's why we are here. But before that, let me order something or else I will die of starvation," she said calling a waiter to serve her. "One café frappe with crushed ice over the top for me and hmm... one café mocha for him. Is my choice for you perfect?"

"I am stepping out of your life Tehzeeb," I replied with no connection to her choice from the menu.

She froze for a moment as she heard this. She nodded to the waiter giving him a signal to move out of the conversation. "But we are friends and there is no reason to lose connection."

"Whether you like or hate Sid, is your issue. I just don't want to hurt my friend."

"So for you only he is important and not me," she said. "All those moments we shared on phone meant nothing to you. I did not think that you would act so cowardly."

When God gives us the freedom of choice; he also makes it tough for us by making us pay heavy prices on account of our choice. When we are free to choose, it's the barriers of choice that play an important role. I felt like a person standing at the edge of a 100 ft deep tube well; no matter what decision I took, I would fall into it. The choice was to be made between two friends and which one to choose.

It was the most difficult decision of my life. I felt helpless to move onto to either side. I took a deep breath and faced Tehzeeb who was looking at me with a peculiar expression on her face. She looked into my eyes for a moment and then hurried out of the café. The tears of women can melt a heart of stone. That day Tehzeeb cried in front of me.

She melted my heart with her emotions breaking the tough layer of friendship, which I had created for Sid.

I promised that I would help her. I will be with her all the time. The spying nature of Sid was a result of his possessiveness and I could bear it no longer. I had to do something to get him out of all this fuss.

Another cold night during the dreadful winter made me move early into my room. I quickly changed and snuggled into the comforts of my woolen blanket.

When I found nothing to do for time-pass, I switched on my Lappy to watch a movie. The only option I had was '*Tere Naam*'. It was a good movie but watching it for the third time was definitely a bad idea. It's rightly said though, "Beggars can't be choosers." I loved the movie for Salman Khan; but I couldn't see him crying with a bald face.

I closed my eyes for a few minutes. Soon sleep conquered my consciousness. Suddenly in my dreams, Sid's bald face appeared. He was crying lying on the floor for his ladylove. Drops were falling from his eyes but he was helpless. It was frightening and disturbing. His face gave me a shock, and I suddenly woke up.

"Why are you sweating brother?" Sid came forward to calm me down.

"I saw a horrible dream. It was bad. I would never let that happen to you."

"Let what happen to me?" He questioned strangely.

"Yeah… I saw you bald inside a rehabilitation center crying for her. You tried to forget her but her memories were ruining your life"

"Are you talking about Tehzeeb?"

"Yes," I nodded.

"I think you have gone insane," he exclaimed.

"What if she didn't love you back? Will you be able to resist your obsession? What if she falls for somebody else? Will you accept the fact and move on with your life?"

My questions didn't leave Sid without a thought. I badly needed the answers not because I was confused between the two; but I was actually worried about Sid's fate, Tehzeeb and of course me in between them.

"If she didn't love me back, I will wait for her till she finds somebody more adorable than me. I will simply move out of her life thinking that it wasn't written in my destiny. But I strongly feel she will love me back one day," he prophesized.

The next day was another ordinary day, except that letter which made Sid sob the whole day. It came straight from his orphanage which mentioned a sudden death of Verma aunty. It was hard to handle Sid. He was shattered because Verma aunty was like a mother to him. I got him a ticket to Mumbai for the rituals. It was going to take almost 14 days for Sid to be back.

The day he went, I kept thinking about the words he had spoken to me. I pushed his words out of my head and instead gave a thought to one of his statements, *"... till she finds somebody more adorable than me; then I will leave her obsession forever."*

If you don't get the drug, it may leave you uneasy for a while; but in the end the addiction simply stops. It was then that I thought of taking control.

It was tough to make Sid believe what Tehzeeb had spoken to me.

The only option was to become that adorable guy of Tehzeeb's, which would make Sid forget her.

I was going to play with a girl's life, but that was the only option I had.

5

A girl is like a rainbow.

A rainbow that is filled with emotions, filled with colors, filled with joys and sorrows. And that is what makes her herself.

She's got different shades; colors with seven different emotional, dynamic and ever changing hues. As you triumph over these; you will see that she will slowly let go off her inhibitions and trust you completely falling into your arms. It's magical. Soon you will realize you have conquered her world. In order to understand her completely, she needs to be sheltered from the rains; protected from the thunder. She needs to feel comfortable with you; it's very important that she trusts you.

Only after she is in the comfort zone will you be able to explore her myriad shades and colors. This is something I have learnt with time. Every girl has a different desire; a different sacrifice; ego, love, attitude, pain and pride. This is all you need to understand; provided that every girl is different in her own sacred way. They all are more or less the same, just like the leaves of a tree; same yet different.

A true mystery, that's what she is.

When I first met Tehzeeb, those million thoughts didn't take over me. What would she be thinking of me? Is she even noticing me? Am I her types? Is she interested in me? etc. I always tried to be myself with the feminine gender. I tried to be as simple as I could. But today was something different. I couldn't imagine to have influenced by those so-called 'love-guides' which were written without experiences, stuffed with an endless number of advices. I knew the universal fact, "Let her not love you for what you pretend to be; or she will be shocked to find an entirely different person in the later stage and she will surely not appreciate that." But still I moved towards the path all filled with a plan to play with the emotions of that pretty girl Tehzeeb.

All I got was 13 days to make Tehzeeb fall in love with me. I soon needed to find her colors of the rainbow, before Sid arrived; bringing his obsession to a halt. Tehzeeb knew that she deserved someone better than Sid, who would take care of her, understand her, respect her and would be ready to do anything for her.

Yes, and that was not me. No one could be as better as Sid for Tehzeeb. Yet, she needed to fall in love with me. I had to lure her into my trap; a master-plan for the trap of love.

I took the challenge of accomplishing this in 13 days.

How to get a girl in 13 days?

Day 1.

I was a little tired from yesterday's exertion and woke up a little later than usual, had a warm bath in the crappy bathroom of my miniscule room and headed downstairs for breakfast; only to find omelet and sandwich again. "Shit!" I muttered. I was sick of this breakfast; that's all I had for the past few weeks. I asked someone for a nice place for breakfast around. I was told there was a South Indian place right around the corner. As I headed that way, I passed the morning market. People were opening their shops hoping for a good business.

I saw this Super Star Saloon just before my destination, Venkat's *Dosas.* The saloon had a cheap picture of Hritik Roshan topless, giving a million dollar smile, wearing those multi-colored goggles! After a few seconds of laughing at it, I realized that I was due for a decent shave and a haircut. I still had a couple of hours before I saw Tehzeeb. I walked in and got rid of that scratchy beard and goofy moustache. My hair was also a messy; it got the desired trimming too.

After the job was done I looked into the mirror and I realized how handsome I had looked once; the recent turn of events had just made me careless about my looks. But after the hair-cutting was done, once again I looked like the old Dev.

After all, I had to make an impression today! The first impression is the last impression. And I seriously required this makeover.

After *vada-sambhar* at Venkat's *Dosas*, I came back to my room and again had a bath to get rid of the itch from the haircut.

As I stood naked in front the mirror I realized that girls like a clean and hygienic guy. This makeover was surely going to impress her. I decided to keep my look neat and sober and always wear clean and tidy clothes for the near future at least.

I have always had a firm belief that having a good posture and physique is also very important in order to get noticed. If the girl sees you from behind and you're standing up straight, with just a slight slouch; she will assume that you are good looking.

Readers, if you're hunched up with your arms folded across your chest and you are walking with your feet slightly inwards, it doesn't matter how hot you really are; girls won't cast a second glance at you. Posture is important.

I had read somewhere, "If you want to get noticed; apply new things to yourself." This got me thinking for myself to show-off. I went to Levi's Fashion in the afternoon to see their latest collection and got a few pairs as they had good designs. I filled my wardrobe with new denims and retro washes ranging from cargos to flat-pocket jeans. I had a total reformation with a spike cut, grey lenses, sporty college casuals and a gymnasium visit on my daily routine. It was much needed.

A fallen needle might go unnoticed; but a nail can't be over looked. I needed to be that nail for Tehzeeb; the nail that pierces into the heart of poor Tehzeeb; the ruthless nail that slashes the insides of Tehzeeb.

I got ready, put on some new, freshly bought clothes and headed to meet Tehzeeb.

Tehzeeb was surprised looking at my new attire. Sheena even touched me to see if I was real. It felt like some kind of a test that I needed to pass.

"Oh, my, God… What have you done with your hair! Look at you, am I day-dreaming or what?" she said while stretching my cheek as if they were made of rubber, making the skin go red. This was one activity that irked me a little. (Attention women! Guys do not like their cheeks being pulled as if they are five year olds; especially when they have dressed up with so much of care for you.) But all was fair, when I was more concerned about what Tehzeeb liked and disliked. There was no groom for personal desires.

"I'm always like that; may be you never noticed before," I said sarcastically.

"Are your parents getting you married?" She asked.

"No, they haven't found anyone in your comparison as yet," I chuckled giving her a compliment.

"*Hai hai…*" she giggled. "You are funny. And hey, I like your new *avatar*."

"I will always keep you laughing like this; I will always be your funny guy. Here I am, your own little stand-up comedian! After all everyone needs a little amusement in their lives. For you, it's me!" I was laying my trap for her.

"Oho, Buddhu!" She smiled again and hugged me. I felt that she would love me after all, looking at my attire.

After some random chats and a few discussions, I left and headed back to my place saying goodbye for the rest of the day. I had to pick up a few things on my way back. I also wanted to visit the book store I had seen earlier this morning while I was going to have breakfast.

I summed up that this whole day had gone in making her interested in me. I had passed the test. I thought of preparing myself to move to the next level. After all, I was fighting the battle here; the battle within and without; the battle between myself and everything else; just for my friend Sid. Coping with the psychological transformation, the physical transformation was much needed; and I had accomplished it just perfectly.

After buying some love-guides I went to my room and called it a day after dinner and an hour of assignment.

Day 2.

The next day I applied my strategies on a more subtle, intellectual level; the idea was to strike a conversation all of a sudden. That was the idea I got from that love-guide book.

It said, "Try not to do this while she's talking to someone or looks like she's in a hurry. This will probably annoy the girl, and minimize your chances of impressing her. Having patience and making your move with caution is the key. After a few exchanged smiles, ask her something unusual. Please don't try out any pick-up lines from our Bollywood movies on her unless they are specifically to make her laugh!"

All I needed was to get her attention. After the brain-numbing lecture by Professor Fatima, I was in no mood to discuss Economics. But in order to get Tehzeeb talking, I had to bring in Fatima as a topic starter.

"So what you think about the professor?" I asked as if I really want to know.

"Think what? She is nice and has great knowledge in the subject of Economics," she said, a little surprised by this sudden question.

"Economic is all what the economists say; there is nothing new about it," I said while Tehzeeb just pondered over the fact.

"Will you help me understand those dangerous Industrial policies of 1977 & 1991?" she said putting on a pleading expression on her charming face. I shook my head as a negation and moved about five paces. She was surprised and shocked at my reaction; but then I turned around and smiled. That was the 'yes' she needed. She was still watching me shyly, laughing over the unsaid joke. She knew I would always be there to help her out.

We talked for hours as I taught her the stupid laws and that the other related stuff. I was satisfied to discover the fact that she understood me. Beauty and brains together - what a package! Just everything a man needs!

We drifted from topic to topic, talking about equations, laws and theories for a few hours. We continued our conversation through a walk as well. It felt wonderful.

After a while, I told her that I will see her later and walked away. I didn't take too much of her time. That way she realized that I respected her individual space.

That night was tough. Tehzeeb was all in my thoughts. "What would be my next move?" I murmured inside, but then I just moved my hands over the book to get more ideas.

Day 3.

I thought of moving to the next step and decided to send her a text. I wanted to know what she had to say about this SMS, "Just got up with a beautiful dream. We are at the café, just the two of us, sipping our favorite coffee. I think morning dreams turn out to be true. Do you think so?"

If she said yes, it would give me the meeting at the café; a meeting that was immediately essential to plant that seed of love. I had my fingers crossed waiting for the text reply that I was eager to read.

'*Buddy, you got a message!*' My cell finally buzzed. Yeah, that was my ringtone!

Anyway, I closed my eyes and prayed for the best, then opened my right eye just a little to read what my mobile had to say. My right eye just needed a glimpse. Oh damn! I quit playing little games with myself, and hurriedly opened both my eyes to read.

I had hit the Jackpot!

"Meet me at d cafe, 10 AM today," I read aloud, making sure the message was true, and then jumped with joy on hearing from her again.

The plan was working. I knew, to keep her interested, I should never play hard to get.

I looked at the watch and realized that it was 9 already. "Fuck!" I cursed myself. I still had to take a bath and get ready. And the drive from my place to the mall was at least 30 minutes. Hurriedly, I got myself ready and I went to the mall. I wondered, "When we live at the same place, why to hire two different modes to reach the same destination." But then I forgot that rule, "Your girl would love to see you waiting; so never be late, rather try to reach as early as possible"

I thought I will be late, but when I looked at the watch, I was actually early. I deliberated over the fact that I will be there before she arrives. I arrived at the meeting place ten minutes earlier; I don't know how I made it work like that.

I was surprised to see her already there, smiling at me. The café was a chaos; it was filled with super hot-shot, beautiful babes. I was in total awe as I saw these girls in all attitudes, shapes and sizes!

Shapes from curvy pears to juicy melons! Yes, they ranged from 'barely there' to 'Oh my God! Are they real?' and please do not get me started on the butt sizes.

But I had work to do; I looked right into her eyes giving her a hundred percent of my attention. The intention was to show her that I was least interested in any of the shapely figures around. It was an unsaid fact about me that I respect every human being. I express this through my nature; no need to put it into words. The same applies to girls; they will surely give you respect if you give them the same.

"Good morning, Tez… you look astonishing." My compliment made her lips stretch into a beautiful smile. I took her hand and greeted her with a kiss. That was a small gesture; but all that mattered was my touch. I noticed the chill that passed her body when I did so and the expression on her face that she very desperately tried to hide; she had just realized that she was exceptionally adorable to my eyes.

"Excuse me," she called a waiter who was busy serving others. As he arrived I quickly prompted, "One café mocha for me and umm…one café frappe with crushed ice over the top for her." I looked at her and asked, "Is my choice perfect for you?"

And after that, all she did was smile, smile and smile some more. That I had impressed her was written all over her face. I had guessed her taste right, and that was a huge bonus.

When you guess someone's choice right, that person instantly connects to you on a very deep level. That is what happened with Tehzeeb today. I gave her shocks after shocks, as I guessed what she liked and disliked. It was a wonderful experience making that special connection with her. They rest of the day went dreaming and suddenly I felt like it was morning. Yes! It was indeed morning and I missed my night shift. I took the cell phone in my hand and gradually found fifteen messages from Tehzeeb. Thank god! They were all forwards.

Day 4.

I took out my guide to learn more interesting tips. Some of them were simply illogical but what caught my attention was the fact I read out loud, "Girls like the guys who have a good sense of humor. Don't let her think that you are least interested in her conversations and keep mum. Don't also speak so much that she gets no time to speak. You have to maintain the balance just right with your little reactions at every little story of hers that she narrates. I always had this thought to make her laugh. I like to make her miss me all the time for those funny jokes that I crack."

I jumped with joy reading that million dollar advice. I identified a situation and made a funny text that only she could identify with. That's how I started an inside joke with her!

That way, she felt included and came closer to me. She felt free while chatting over the phone. It also gave me an easy-to-come-up-with conversation starter. Days were moving fast and I was waiting for to create an impact on her. I realized that I was happy after a really long time. I was happy because after all this time, I was getting what I wanted.

The whole day passed by with regular conversations, long walks and occasional jokes. I was making her laugh and I was watching her getting closer to me. As she got more comfortable with me, I took my funny sides to different levels and made her realize the value of a good, happy and fun-loving person.

Day 5.

I woke up this morning and rushed directly to the mess. I was damn hungry. As I reached my destination, I was thoroughly surprised to see Tehzeeb. She was dressed in blue and green. "What a beauty," I murmured. I took my plate and filled that with a yellow lump and *Puri*. While moving over to Tehzeeb, my eyes watched a few instances of the famous so-called reality show '*Emotional Attyachar*'. And man, I realized that making her jealous is the best way to get her closer to you.

I have seen that girls get annoyed quickly at sudden and weird changes. Suddenly, I ignored her till the afternoon; didn't talk to her, didn't reply to her text and didn't respond to her calls. She became so desperate to talk to me that she couldn't resist. She must have thought that there is another girl in my life; obviously, she was jealous.

So I ignored her and made her more jealous. While I was gossiping with the hot chicks of the class; I noticed her looking at me with an angry face.

After a whole afternoon of me ignoring and avoiding and she bursting with jealousy; I suddenly went to see her after the classes were over. I guessed that she would be a little mad at me.

As I went to see her at the canteen, she stood up and started walking. I sprang to action and held her hand stopping her from leaving like that. She stopped. She said, "Go to your girlfriends, why would you come to me?"

I said, "no matter how much I talk to others, all I think about is you… and you know that!"

That's it, that's all she needed to hear. She was all happy for the rest of the day and came even closer to me. She started developing a trust in me which assured her that no matter whom I talked to, I was always thinking of her and her only. That's all a girl needs; someone responsible and trustworthy.

But in reality, I was someone entirely different.

Day 6.

I knew, Tehzeeb and I were very different from each other. But we had many similarities as well. My next strategy was to respect those differences and convert them into similarities.

We went out, had lunch together and this whole time, I was like her hero. I had been at her disposal the whole morning. I ordered the food and I stood in line to get stuff. I was the apple of her eye now. I was doing things just to make her happy; something that Sid had never done.

I asked her for a movie after lunch. She was taken aback because we had watched that movie before with the group. She hesitated a little when I asked her; but after seeing me treat her like a princess for the whole day, she agreed happily.

Her acceptance was a 'thumbs-up' to me. Now I could take the scene to the next level.

The movie wasn't really interesting, but my talks kept her busy. In the scary moments, she would hold my hand and shut her eyes tightly in fear. I didn't leave her for a single moment; she never felt alone and uncomfortable.

After the movie I realized that our relationship had moved to a whole new level. It wasn't just friendship anymore.

I wanted to make her fall in love with me. It was the toughest task for me and the most unpredictable one, for you never know how a girl's mind works at times. You can never guess when the task will be accomplished. The instance that one falls in love cannot be exacted; you can only make the surrounding environment conducive for the emotions to soar high and the sparks to start flying. Like they say, you may take the horse to the water; but you can't make it drink.

In my case however, finally I was watching her falling into my trap. My plan was succeeding. She was coming closer and closer to me.

Day 7.

It was the seventh day and I devoted each coming day to the path of making Tehzeeb fall in love. It was another natural day but what occupied students was the test that Prof Fatima was going to take. Every single student was tensed over the fact that the results would be accountable. Tehzeeb was worried and I could easily see fret painted all over her face. I wanted to make her free from the tensed environment which she carried away. What I could probably do was pass a chit, just in case she might read and get her mind diverted.

For the non-*kavis* like me, the next best thing I could do was to write a worst possible poetry for her. I read in the guide book that, "The best way to impress a girl is to show her how much you are concerned about her; doesn't matter even if you fail to be successful."

I have never tried my hands on poetry in my life, but it was easy to write her a bad one.

The sun says to its sunlight, the moon speaks to its moon light,

I'm alone in this beautiful world without you, that's why I need you buddy!

My parents are a part of this world; I'm a part of my parents.

There should be someone from my part, that's why I need you buddy!

I made her feel on the ninth cloud because of me. It was really weird but it made her feel important in my eyes. It made her feel beautiful. I made her feel as if it was only her that I was thinking about all the time, every second, and every moment. I made her feel that she had taken over my mind even in this crucial moment. That is all I needed, to proceed to my next set of plans.

That is the most fascinating and irritating thing at the same time about girls; until you don't make her feel like she's on top of the world; she is not going to care about you.

Day 8.

This was a day of surprises. I gave her a gift that I had bought from the mall earlier. It was this small little keychain with a pink heart that opens and closes as you press the button. It was beautiful and I was sure she would like it. It was very expensive but I had to spend a few bucks in order to keep her from getting away from me.

Again later in the afternoon, I entertained and enticed her by passing secret notes with naughty comments in the middle of the lecture; she was not going to forget these little moments that I was creating in her life. She smiled all the way. I had proved to her that I could do weird things as well; that I was not predictable and that I could be as impulsive and whimsical as her if I was in the mood. I always acted as a funny guy for her.

The guide quoted, "Most girls do not like serious men. But you must try to ask her about studies, material notes and subjects. That way she will feel that you are intelligent and you can help her when she needs it. She will fall for whatever you say and begin to believe what you have to say."

Now it was time for me to move to my next step tomorrow.

Day 9.

Tehzeeb always liked my gestures and responded with an equal number of her gestures to whatever I did. I wish I could know that girl more deeply. I had accomplished too much already in such a short span of time. But that wasn't enough.

I talked about topics where she could involve herself and give her opinions too. She did feel that I always considered what she had to say.

Readers, just because you are a cricket fan, don't start off as a commentator if she hates cricket. Talk about something she likes. Show interest in whatever she talks to you about. You can do this either by cross questioning her or by giving confident consent to her words. Always keep an eye contact. Whenever your eyes meet pass on a simple smile. Give a nod of approval. She will see that you are actually listening to her. She will be happy and satisfied.

All I had was just 4 days in front of me to make this work. It was too less to make her fall in love with me, love that I will later deceive.

Day 10.

We ended up talking for 3 hours straight and didn't even notice the time pass by.

Hand in hand we walked in the garden outside the disc with Tehzeeb's giggles echoing in my ears. Her steps matched mine.

As we walked ahead she said, "I am a lucky girl. Life has been very kind to me. You know since my childhood, I have had enough money to feed and educate myself. I have been lucky to have such caring parents and now I am lucky, in fact luckier, to get a person like you."

I couldn't say the same thing about my family and my life. She already knew everything. I kept telling her about the difficulties I had faced.

She was extremely beautiful. Her nails painted red with cute little hearts on them pressed against the skin of my hand. She was making it impossible for me to think straight.

I thought of building up a romantic atmosphere. I knew '*Woh lamhe...from Jal..'* was her favorite track. I tuned my vocal to her favorite track. As she heard me, she smiled all of a sudden looking at me. "Hey! That is my favorite song!" she said and started start singing along. I told her that it was my favorite too. I knew that in this way, she would think of me whenever she heard that song.

Day 11.

It was the eleventh day. My heart started beating heavily as the sound of a pendulum. I have reached to a stage where in asking her out was the toughest propositions to make. Since last two days I was keen on gathering that gut which would ignite me to act brave and ask that hand. However, nothing was impossible for me now; I had already accomplished so much in a matter of just 10 days. It was now time to take my relationship to a more serious level. I thought of calling her at the café but that wasn't on my chart. A romantic drive with dinner at the Taj was more like my style. It seemed perfectly easy at first, but as I moved towards doing it, it felt so fearful; I almost develop cold feet. It was only me who knew how difficult it was to convince *Shakeel bhai* for that car. I almost grounded myself on his feets to get the jackpot key. God was surly on my side.

I finally decided on taking her for a nice dinner to a good hotel.

On my way I remembered those beautiful lines which made me move to the undecided path, "Enough of those silly lunches and coffees in restaurants and cafes; take her for a candle-light dinner. That will impress her and show her that you have a great taste when it comes to ambience. She will be in your arms in no time if you pull this off correctly."

For guys who want to be a hero in her eyes, check this out. If you think you have the guts to ask her straight, think again; you surely still need some practice like I did.

I relaxed, took a deep breath, exhaled slowly and looked confident; even if I wasn't! No woman likes a man who stutters and stammers while asking her out on a date. I asked her casually for a ride.

Do not hit on her directly. Don't ask, "Would you like to go out with me?" Any woman would be taken aback at this sudden suggestion and may back out much to your dislike.

"I was going to the airport, would you mind joining me," I told her that it was outside the city so we would have a long drive as well. "Hope you didn't have lunch," I asked casually just in case she might had it earlier.

I was specific about my plans as I didn't want to leave her clueless as to where I was going to take her. So I clearly mentioned about the Taj right in the beginning. This made her comfortable with my idea.

I was looking into her eyes waiting for that approval. Though the date demanded bunking of lectures, I wasn't sure she would be comfortable doing that. I thought to insist, but then I didn't repeat.

All thanks to that book which said, "Never push her if she is hesitant. You may blow off another chance that may be lurking around the corner. Have patience and wait as there is always a next time. She will definitely say 'yes', once she has developed that confidence in you. But it may take some time."

It's not as bad as it seems when she says 'no'; I knew there is always a next time; so I waited for the right moment.

I reminded myself not to lose heart when she said 'No'. I knew she longed to come but the lectures took the intentions away. But her denial didn't stop me from asking her out again in the evening for dinner. I needed to make her feel surrounded by the charm I was spreading and that she could take her own time. Strong decisions like this one can never be taken impulsively.

Lucky for me that she agreed to go out with me and we had a fabulous evening. It wasn't Taj but a very authentic food serving restaurant – 'Yellow Chilies' owned by the well-known Sanjeev kapoor. It was as if we had been dating for ages. The food was amazing and she loved it. She wanted to walk along with me but I didn't permit her to do so; it was my idea of taking her out and I will take care of this. It was already late and the gates for our hostel closed at 10pm. I made the ride back to the hostel on time. She was impressed that I could take her to such a nice place.

That night she didn't sleep, nor did I. "Love was in the air… love was really in the air, but it was unsaid though those short messages passing through the satellites."

Day 12.

The day brought new hopes. Might be Tehzeeb was thinking about me, me and only me when I got as many as 20 messages from 'hi' to 'See me as soon as possible". Finally it was time to figure out those end results which would clearly indicate if she liked me or not. It wasn't an easy job to know her heart. She was nurtured well by nature and it came to her naturally to shower lavish affection and care. That was in her genes.

The love guide said, "If a woman you like pampers you like a baby, don't take it for granted and rubbish it away as her overtly caring attitude. If she goes out of her way to make you feel special, then there may be chances that she really likes you. A woman gives strong yet subtle signs that she loves you. Look for those signs."

The following two days I just noticed her reactions. Whenever I passed a compliment, her cheeks turned pink.

Readers, if she blushes when you are around, it mean that she is smitten by you.

My public display of affection was creating wrong vibes in Sheena's mind. Even Tehzeeb was not always comfortable with it I guess. But then sometimes the way she looked at me with those dreamy inviting eyes; they made me feel like she didn't mind me expressing my feelings publicly. That left me quite flattered.

Her body language had changed noticeably when I sat with her now. She would touch my shoulders to get my attention, sometimes rest her palm on mine halfway through a conversation. That was a clear sign that she was getting comfortable with me physically, as the days passed by.

When we went out together, it felt like a fairy came out of her; she looked that beautiful and charming because she took extra care to look good. I told her that she looked sensuous in her outfits because she possessed a combination of simplicity and elegance.

The way she smiled and laughed at my jokes with that extra

attention made me realize; she definitely had a soft corner for me.

From that time, Tehzeeb and I came closer to each other. So close that words weren't necessary to speak to each other now. And yet we talked for hours and hours. It was just my cell balance which reminded me of my lavishness when it came to calling her up. She started avoiding calls from her parents during our conversations. I knew for sure that I was being given more importance than others, which was a direct road to my destination of being loved.

She always encouraged me to go forward with my nerdy plans and always chipped in good advice for me to move ahead in my personal and professional life; I believed she was definitely an ideal lover. I felt that she had just started spending some extra time with me, helping me in all possible ways. The willingness to sacrifice was a clear answer to know if she loved me or not. She would go that extra mile to make me happy, even if that meant sacrificing her hobby. When I looked at chicks, she used to get jealous. Although the feeling of jealousy was not good; it gave an indication that she was now afraid of losing me. Worrying about your safety and whereabouts is one thing through which women often show their love and care. She felt in the same way, knowing for sure that I was her special one.

By now I was experiencing all those signs which proved that she really liked me. For me more than anything else, it was important to respect her emotions; but it was also only me who knew that I was simply playing with them.

Sid was the only thought in my mind and I felt no hesitations inside and planned to speak out my mind to her.

Who knows? I may be in for a pleasant surprise!!

Day 13.

This was the last scene of my whole play and I was on stage performing the climax. I was playing the lead role of my own life and a villain's role in others' lives. But I couldn't care enough. This was my only chance and I had to grab it by the neck. My killer instinct was on the roll for today. I had to do this now; or it would be too late.

Propose to her. Girls like guys proposing to them in some style and not telling 'the thing' straight away. Even if she refuses or tells you that she needs time, remember to respect her feelings.

My final jackpot was the Taj and I was well prepared to show my aces. She had agreed to go out with me again and this was the only chance I had. As we entered we were greeted by a pretty lady in her early twenties.

"How may I assist you," she said politely.

"Could you arrange us a table for two," I said. She took us to one of the corner table but then I insisted to make special arrangements in the middle. The words made Tehzeeb smile and hold my hand. As we reached I said her to order stealing two minutes from our precious date for the loo.

It was a day before Sid was going to arrive…

"Could I have everyone's attention for a few seconds please?" I said rather loudly. Everyone looked at me to see what was more important than the food served there. Even Tehzeeb turned her head towards the voice from where it was coming. Her mouth left open when she saw me.

"I've been with this lovely girl Tehzeeb for the last two years and I have never felt so wonderful like the way I've felt for the past few days. I wanted to tell everyone how much I love this girl and how much she means to me." Everyone applauded, hooted and shouted out their appreciation to that and I smiled.

"I mean we've only been going out for the last few days; but nothing seems as special to my eyes as this beautiful lady!!!" I continued as I went down on one knee and was struggling to get my hand out of my pocket. You could tell that I was nervous. I pulled out a red rose and a ring.

She was stunned; why wouldn't she be? She just gawked at the rose. Everyone around us gasped too at what I was doing.

"Tez… you're the most beautiful, charming, caring, forgiving, loving, smart and just simply a wonderful woman. I loved you the first day when you thanked me for losing the debate and I loved you even more from the day you gave me that card. I want to make you happy and never let you down, feel any sorrows or sadness. May I have the honor of asking your hand for this ring?" I said so confidently and so beautifully.

She was just astonished; she didn't know what to say. She just had one hand covering her mouth.

Then the unexpected happened. She snapped me out of my daze, grabbed my hand and started walking out of the room with me in tow.

"Is this a no?" I asked sadly.

"I don't know Dev. It's a big day. To be honest I don't know what to say," she said sincerely. I looked at her; she had rejection written all over her face and sadness in her eyes.

"I couldn't say no, nor could I say a yes," she whispered.

"But you cannot deny the fact that you like me," I said. She didn't deny that but was rather afraid of the consequences.

Finally I had the fish inside my net. Mission accomplished.

With a wide smile and moist eyes, she hugged me and accepted my proposal.

We walked back into the dining room; thank goodness everyone was already eating and not looking at us. We hurriedly left the place for our college. It was already too much and I don't know how much more she could take.

The next day was a little lazy. The morning poured in through the windows; it felt like the golden glory of the sun was drenching us.

There was something special in the air.

The classes were boring and I had those 'Industrial policies' as a reason to make Tehzeeb bunk. Tehzeeb did fail in the exam as my stupid poetry kept buzzing around. I headed towards my room hiding Tehzeeb from the hostel guards.

"I'm sorry I got tea for you, but it spilled," she batted her eyelashes and smiled innocently at me.

I looked like I was going to laugh, but I tried to hide it as much as possible. "Well don't worry; we will go to the café after studying," I said.

My room was messy. I quickly grabbed those playboy magazines and the clothes to dump somewhere. I knew Tehzeeb had already looked over the stuff but then I acted innocent sliding all the blame on Sid.

It was now, only me and Tehzeeb inside the room while the whole hostel was busy attending lectures. The two opposite sexes alone in a room is always questionable. But at no point of time did I let this guilt of sex emerge in her mind. I wanted to be in my limits. May be that was not in my plan or may be that was not at all in my dictionary. I could play mentally but never had I thought that would anytime turn physical. Tehzeeb was lying besides me and I was getting uncomfortable. Realizing this I rose from my bed and stood up; but then suddenly Tehzeeb stood up and closed the door. I heard a click when she locked the door.

"I'm sorry Tez... I won't, be able to... you know... what you trying to..?" My words stopped when suddenly she took both my hands and raised them above my head; then slowly descended closer to my face. She drew me close and pushed me against the wall with a soft smile on her lips. I knew that she could trust me blindly; that I would never hurt her no matter what happened. She knew that I loved her as much as she did; maybe even more if that was even possible. But that was all she knew; all the falsehood I darted over her life.

It was at that moment; I lost all my thoughts, all my senses and stood in front of her, as vulnerably as a guy can standing in front of a girl he truly loves. I looked into those beautiful eyes which had seemed to touch my heart for the first time; right now they were burning. I now realize the beauty of Tehzeeb painted over Sid. I was scared enough to feel myself fall for that beauty. Her eyes were alight with fire. Consumed by them, my eyes began to reflect her fire; I seemed to forget everything. Her touch was tender; yet possessive and passionate. Her hands on either side of my neck sent shivers down my spine. I pressed her against the wall and then pressed myself into her. My hands rested on the wall with her in between.

She smelled fabulous. I had always been fascinated by perfumes. They were like a message, which did not need a language to convey what their wearer had to say. I could be deaf and mute or an alien from the outer space; yet I was sure I would identify the fragrances which came directly from Tehzeeb. It was turning me on. That perfumes contained an irrational and mysterious element which force me to act her way.

She kissed me soft and slow. Her lips touched mine and then retreated again for a quick catch of breath. Her thumb rested on my lower lip pulling it open ever so slightly so she could enter me. It was such a sweet kiss that I felt myself going gooey; my heart melting. My hands fisted in her hair drawing her closer, pulling her further into my confines until we were totally lost in each other, becoming a single entity.

I pulled the zip of her hot pink parka down till her waist, and slid my fingers inside the long sleeves. Touching her made my heartbeats go crazy.

My lips moved down kissing the hollow of her neck. She moaned as a hot electric desire coursed through her body. I wanted her... I wanted her badly.

"Tehzeeb," I whispered, my breath ragged and voice husky, "Are we doing anything wrong?"

As an answer to my question she kissed me; my tongue entwined with hers passionately. The meaning couldn't have been any clearer. I never knew that it was possible to love someone so much or to be loved so completely. She made me forget everything; she made me forget myself. I opened the clasp of her bra and nudged the straps down.

I looked at her. Shadows fell over her face. Her hair was messed up; mostly my doing. She placed her palms on my chest under my shirt. She laughed looking at my chest hair and with that naughty smile and twinkling eyes, she won me over. There were times, even after having spent so much of time together when I still couldn't believe that she was mine; with me, for me. It seemed like a fantasy too good to be true.

Suddenly there were footsteps in the corridor. Who could be here at this time? I could hear them coming closer and closer and then the door knob turned.

The door knob turned and I gasped.

"Dev..! Are you inside?" A voice came from the other side of the door. Another knock and I got so frightened that I felt like somebody had taken the soul out of me.

Standing on the other side of the door was Sid who had just came back from his orphanage. I completely forgot his plans of coming back to college. What was scaring me was the thing that I had just got myself into; it was too big to hide from him. I quickly switched off the lights and made Tehzeeb hide inside my wardrobe.

"Hey man welcome back," I said rubbing my eyelids pretending to have been woken up suddenly from sleep. A yellow beam of light darted across the floor. Though the light flooded in from the window, most of the room was still in darkness. I was pretty sure that Sid hadn't a clue about what had just happened in this very room.

"How come you are here and not in class?" He questioned.

"Was not feeling good so thought I'd rest," I said and then

changed the topic quickly by saying, "Sid, you need to rush to Professor Fatima urgently."

"Anything serious?" He questioned before leaving the room and heading towards the staff room, on discovering that I didn't know.

I thanked the Almighty a thousand times for getting me out of the mess without thinking out the reason to answer Sid back.

As I opened the wardrobe, Tehzeeb came out coughing loudly. She bent down to catch her breath and then started yelling at me for not reminding her about Sid's arrival.

A couple of months passed by and my relationship with Tehzeeb grew stronger and deeper. We went on occasional dates, hiding from Sid and spent whatever little time we had with each other. My feelings towards her were growing stronger with every minute I spent on her and differences with Sid grabbed equal pace. He knew that there was something fishy going around with me and Tehzeeb.

"Might be, Sheena filled his ears," I thought. I was scared many times but I never gave up. I said "I love you" every morning and every night; she thought that if I didn't say it, something would be missing and that her heart might break.

I was waiting for the right moment to disclose things to my group mates and the coming fresher's party was my chance. I was afraid inside about how Sid would feel. The only thing which kept me steady was his words, "I will quit desiring her if she falls for anybody and that includes even you, Dev."

His words kept ringing in my ears from the day I touched Tehzeeb to the fresher's party where I was going to make my false love public.

6

I was about to sleep.

I had arranged the pillows well, lit the night lamp and the books were kept in the wall niche.

As I got into bed and stretched myself yawning myself to sleep, my cell phone beeped and I stood up. After a tiring day of studies and lectures I generally keep my phone on silent; but today I had forgotten. I hate their buzzing idiotic sounds; but when it buzzed twice, I thought I'd give a look.

I saw the screen and it said

Sender: 9998477235 with a

'Hi there! Can we be text-mates?'

Not knowing who the sender was I deleted the message right away and placed the phone under the pillow, placing my wrist over the forehead; I closed my eyes to sleep.

Again the bugger buzzed!

Sender: 9998477235

'Hi! You still awake, I know this. Care 2 b my text-mate?'

(This time the disturbing message ended with a stupid frowning smiley at me; as if the sender had done some great research on when I sleep and when I am awake.)

I thought aloud, "Who the hell could this be asking for being the text-mate in the wee hours of the night when legally wed and beloved are having their share of the greatest pleasures in the world?"

Damn the sender!

I was never a 'text maniac'. My parents gave me this toy so that they could monitor me even if they were miles away. I wanted to switch off the gadget, but that day my mother wanted to speak late night as she had messaged me earlier.

This text thing was annoying me. Just as I was about to close my eyes and return to my dreamless sleep, the phone beeped again.

Same number...!

Such determination! Oh gosh!

'Please reply to this message & be an angel & save me from falling into abyss.'

The message struck me. I got up and started punching the keys. I just realized I was replying to the message.

'You! Who is it? Look, I'm not an angel, and if you want

someone to save you, then it's definitely not me. I'm just a simple person whom you have been successful in waking up at this hour of the night! Stop these immature pranks and kindly fuck off. Anyway, just by any chance do I know you?' – Message sent.

Tick tick tick.... seconds later I got the reply.

'Nope! You don't know this lonely soul. Nor does she know you well. But she wants to be your friend; a good friend.'

'Ahh! Good friend? Then it is perfectly fine. It's Dev here; but how did you get my number?' I replied.

'Hi Dev, I'm not any prankster, trust me!' her message was laden with emotion which carried me away, but I wasn't too sure to trust it blindly.

'But how did you get my number, speak up,' I demanded.

'Remember two days back you came to our class for making an announcement of this upcoming, interesting, fun filled fresher party? By the way, I am a female. I thought I had already given you the hint in the last message?'

I had gone to as many as 9 classes where I had to announce about the fresher's. It was tough to find the bug that had sneaked into my hair at this time of the night. It's strange to meet people on phone but she seemed interesting. I did give a second thought that she might be Tehzeeb. But Tehzeeb wouldn't play pranks. She knew me very well. It couldn't be Sid too, as he was snoring besides me.

We ended up exchanging messages and learned quite a lot about each other that night. She was lovely, poetic and a lot more. Her words were trustworthy and I gradually drifted away with the charm she showered on me. Her words were like an echo, a saccharine echo to my ears which only left sweet melodies. We said goodbye only to realize that it was sharp 6 am in the morning.

She had the power to drive the sleep away from my eyes which I had realized in a day itself. I had never received such attention in my life and I wanted to know how far this could get me.

Sunlight spilled over my blanket. The sun rays felt like a silken cloth giving me a smooth touch. The excitement of that new girl had left me sleepless for a night. I had my bath and got ready for class. The remaining day turned to a routine but the obvious shadows under my eyes caused by the lack of sleep, might have invited comment; so I thought of putting on a pair of sunglasses. They were the kinds that magically darken in bright light. I had bought them that summer, and I wore them hoping that when she was looking at me (she knew my identity, and I still didn't know how she looked), I would pass off as a dude to her. Sunglasses go well with thick, dark hair like mine anyway.

'The echo of your laughter is all over the campus. Come upstairs and share it with me. I also want to laugh with you,' a message beeped while I was in the campus gossiping with Sheena, teasing her about her weight.

I called on the number.

No response.

She neither called back nor picked up my call.

There was something about her that was making me insane. I didn't even know her name but one thing was sure; she was from the same college, so finding her wasn't problematic.

I played a trick on Sid thinking it would be him.

"I caught; I caught 'HER' Sid!"

"Who is this beauty?"

"It is none other than YOU, my beauty!" I chuckled at the lame proposition I was making.

"How come?"

"Look, despite of calling from various numbers, she doesn't pick up. Something makes me think she doesn't want to reveal her masculine voice to me. It was you who played the trick. I know you, you prankster! I know you!"

"No Dev, why would I do this? Let's call the customer care number and check who it is."

"Deal."

"How much will you give me?"

"Shall gift you the love of Tehzeeb in return," I said.

"What a naughty boy… Ahem! Ahem! You are in love with that new girl, Dev?"

"I don't know…come on, Sid! You know me well….right?"

"That's the reason I asked because I know you so well. I am trying to find out whom you love."

"Oh! Not again," I sighed for a zillionth time as Sid took over and did things he felt were best for me.

"It is somebody whose age is fifty-four and her name is Maria D'souza; but couldn't cross check if this was true because of the infidelity issues that most women are facing today in the world."

"What? Are you serious? 54? No wonder she sounded so caring and concerned about me..." I wondered out loud, then embarrassed, looked at Sid. There was a moment of silence and then we both burst out laughing. We had the laugh of the day discovering our darling Aunty '*Dee soo zaa*'.

Sid laughed every now and then suggesting, "It might be an old widow who got your number and has rediscovered her long lost teenage, thanks to you Dev; all those buried libidinal instincts that she swept the carpet, you are helping her unearth them. What do you think, Dev?"

"You are kidding me!" I said but Sid suggested not to text her again. The matter was soon buried, but my inquisition got that out of the graveyard. My head and heart spoke two different languages and so this time I didn't follow Sid's advice. It was a new beginning whose end could wreak havoc in my life but my heart at the moment, was not thinking about the price I would have to pay.

A day would not pass by without a loving and thoughtful message from her. She taught me to appreciate the beauty and romance of text messages and I now became eager and excited every time my phone beeped, hoping that it would be her. But on the other hand I was slowly realizing that what I had done intentionally to Tehzeeb was something that I shouldn't have done. Today I was in a position where my heart longed for the text girl but my head was keeping me in check with thoughts of Tehzeeb, Sid and everything that I had gotten myself into.

I thought of not replying, but her response sent shivers down my spine, *'Value the people who have touched your life because you will never know just when they will walk out & never come back again.'*

I replied,

'Don't come close if later you will go away;

Don't touch me if later you will shy away;

Don't love me if later you will leave me crying...

Separation in my case is quite a possibility and this anticipation in contradiction to the union of two souls would definitely leave you devastated and with a pain which would be unbearable. Would you be able to bear this?'

Despite my denying her in these long texts on my 3.5 X 4.5 cm screen; she kept sending messages and quotes. Hopeless, silly love quotes from many coffee table books, verses from classic text books where some great poets like Shakespeare's or Longfellow's legendary verses must have been published I didn't know. All I could say was that all the messages she sent me were wonderful; they came from the heart and the mind always has problems trying to forget the forbidden fruit. This made me alert enough to not think of taking the relationship any further.

But when nothing goes right, take a left turn.

Whenever I asked her when we would meet in person, she always answered, "Soon... soon... soon." Not seeing each other did not lessen my feelings for her in any way; rather what I felt for her grew deeper and stronger each day.

And I was sure that she felt the same way too. Text messages were the only proof of her existence and I could only speculate about her facial features, her height, limbs, her lips and many other things that I dreamt about. I couldn't think any more; not enough to make me erotic or elated. On one hand I was now desperate to see her; on the other I was on check due to my self-talks on the norms I had set for myself to remain the same old 'Mumma's boy' and 'Dad's budding blossom'. I told myself that this isn't falling in love but there was definitely something that drove me crazy.

I felt like being taken for a ride and I felt like she was avoiding me. It was still strange that she never picked up my calls when I tried calling. As soon as I chose not to reply though, she threw a tantrum and always ended up convincing me with her laconic vocabulary.

Such determination and conviction drew me towards her. Was she trapping me into the web of love?

For the first time in my life, I felt that my mood would depend on the messages I got as a reply from her. If she could control my life with her absence, then what would happen if she makes me feel her presence?

In the due course of time however, I didn't know what to do. I didn't want to lose her. I had learned to love her and I wanted to be with her forever even if I did not know how she looked. I thought of questioning her if she was feeling the same as I was.

Co-incidentally, that night, she sent me this message, '*Loving you secretly is a hard thing for me to do; hoping, wondering if you will feel the same way. But even I can't read your mind if you love me or not. Whatever it is, I'll still love you and I hope the same...*'

By that time we had been exchanging messages for more than a month. God knew how happy I was. She was right. Although we had not seen each other, what we felt was enough to make us both realize what was keeping us together.

'*I wish I could really tell you how much you mean to me, but I'm afraid to love, scared to get hurt. I am afraid of committing to anyone dear. Listen, I hope you understand me. And as a good pen friend I wish you get the best person to be with. You must be a good girl I am sure. Be the same forever.*' Another text message from me and our lives took different turns.

'*I wish to take the right turn, Dev. I wish at least that we will meet one fine day and I am sure of that. I wanted you to like me for what I am and rather not judge me by my outer appearances.*

That's why I value this relationship so much; for even if we haven't seen each other, we still have deep feelings for each other. Hope you are not messing around with another girl.'

'I hope you will soon meet me and 'soon' means 'soon'! But I also hope that you will not get tired of loving me the same way you do now. I wish to speak the truth though it may hurt you. And do you know what? This truth hurts me too, dear. You are smart enough to understand what I am conveying, right?' I responded to her message.

'Are you already in a relationship? If no then think again, Dev, think again!'

Her message made me think about the recent events in my life; about what importance I was giving other human beings and my relationship with them. It really made me think about Tehzeeb and this messenger of 'love-lick-ice-candy' messages. I was now forced to weigh them both in my eyes and a warm sentiment of dilemma gripped my nerves and all of a sudden I had shivers running down my spine. What would a boy do when he is at crossroads with two girls? What does he do when his basic approach to life begins with the avoidance of relationships?

I never really had one like her ever in my life. She was right though. It was the college lifestyle and the peer pressure that was catching on to me; once college ended, I would be out of this whole 'falling in love' syndrome. I was still in a dilemma. How could 'love' happen to me?

I secretly dated Tehzeeb and still couldn't manage to announce about the relation publicly. How was I supposed to handle two relationships? I was fiddling with two lives. Oh, my God! I was not realizing; was not even aware of what was happening inside me and what I was doing to people.

Love messages continued to flow through our phones, between our hearts, which made us go through each day with the thought that sooner or later, on a fine day, we would see each other, face to face, heart to heart.

It was a dull day. The next lecture was after an hour. I went to the library to kill time. Tehzeeb too turned up at the library with Sheena. She looked beautiful in that single piece she was wearing.

I said, "Hi!" But Tehzeeb didn't respond. She ignored me going back to whatever she was doing on the far side of the desk.

I also showed myself busy with other stuff. I guess our relation now needed some fertilizer to grow.

Again a message came from the same number.

'Though we are a few steps apart,

You are always in my heart.

I close my eyes & there you are!

Even if I never see you,

I'll always be there to care for you,

Much longer than forever...'

For a moment I was scared of Tehzeeb being the text girl; but then I looked around and found her searching through books. I called the number just to give a check; but no reply. My impatient fiddling with the mobile, the smile on my face and then this cross checking; all of this definitely must have made Tehzeeb wonder that there was something fishy.

She quickly turned and stared at my face. "So you thought you could act smart with me? Come on Dev, you should know by now whom you're messing with."

I just stared back at her making sure I showed her no emotions. She questioned me as many as fifty times about my strange behavior but all I could tell her was a lie.

I was feeling like the stuffing of a homemade grilled sandwich.

I moved to the class leaving all thoughts aside. I requested the professor to give me permission to rest in class. My head was aching like anything; I was sure even a Disprin wouldn't have worked. I slammed my head on the desk creating a thudding noise in the middle of the lecture. I didn't want to look up. I already knew that most of the people surrounding me were staring at me. I just kept my head down on my desk until class was over. The entire time in class I was wondering what I should do with my life.

After the professor dismissed us, I was the first one out of the door. My next class wasn't until three, so I had plenty of time after lunch.

I thought of calling that text girl to refresh my mind. After one ring she answered, "Hey baby! How are you? How was your day?"

(Yes, by now we had progressed to telephonic conversations.)

"Baby?" I asked her wondering to myself, "Do I look like that?"

"My day was horrible. I'm tired and agitated. How was your day?", I tried to sound as sweet as I could, but ended up sounding the exact opposite of the intended, especially after that comment.

"It was horrible," I sounded so depressed.

"Why? What happened? Something went wrong?" Worry engulfed the truly love-sick girl.

"I didn't get to see you. I miss you," I sounded like I had lost a part of her.

"Awww..... I miss you too…" This day was crazy.

"Well, I'm at the library; you can join me if you like," I said as sweetly and tantalizingly as possible.

"Library? Isn't it too early in the year to be at the library?" She sounded skeptical.

"Yeah, I was doing my assignment and I want to get rid of it as soon as possible."

"I see. I would love to join you with all my heart but today doesn't sound very good," she said.

"What is wrong with the date?"

"How about the fresher's party? We will have fun, meet each

other, experience the joy of the wonders we have created so far. Honestly, even I want to see you… feel…"

"Soon then; love ya…bubbayie…" I said and kept the phone. The magic of her love had made me blind and deaf; I was now incapable of thinking about the plan I already had for the fresher's. Tehzeeb and me were going to confess and disclose our love publicly.

But when the text-girl asked me to join her at the fresher's party the coming weekend, I got super excited, pushing aside all thoughts about Tehzeeb. I began swapping my wardrobe possessions with my friends on the D-day. A black trouser seemed perfect with that new shaved look of mine and my inherent sharp features. With it, a royal violet shirt with the exclusive tag of 'Raymond' would make me worthy of the salutation, "Gentleman, how are you?" I wore the best of my gogs bought from Ray Ban though I knew it wasn't summer; nor would the floor be flashing lights at me.

I wondered why the occasion of meeting a girl was not a matter of coincidence in my life. I wondered why I hadn't been dashed by a girl in the corridors and then fallen for her *lehrati zulfein*, her lucky lips or her *nashilee ankhien*. I wondered about every possible thing I could before meeting my beloved; the pleasure of whose touch I had never had.

The party was jazzed up with hot babes and dudes in black, white and red fit the retro style. With a scarf around the neck, Goan caps and snazzy belts, the chicks could be seen swirling their glasses while talking and laughing without a worry in this world.

There I found my Tehzeeb, no, Sid's Tehzeeb, who came and stood by my side. She stared at me with an expression I understood only too well. I had to give her my hand for the 'Romeo rocks' number blaring out of the stereo and join her on stage with the DJ who was rocking the party.

I said, "I won't dance, Tehzeeb. I am waiting for a friend of mine here."

But her cajoling made me go her way and with mock frustration and a pair of raised eyebrows on my face, I said, "Okhay!"

"Then let's go." She pulled me along with her.

I was afraid of even holding her by the waist at that moment. But for Tehzeeb, I was her only man. She was dressed purely to lure the handsome. Mind you, I did not add an 's' to the handsome. What a lady she was! Such a perfect match for Sid, I thought. But Sid was somewhere else with the other girls, with his eyes undoubtedly on Tehzeeb and me. This was the fifth song I was dancing with Tehzeeb and the discotheque suddenly turned to a ballroom; the DJ began to play all old remixed numbers, the 20th century hits!

"Hi Dev… Remember me?"

"Ohw! Ow.. Hi!"

I was completely in awe of the woman who had just approached me. She looked amazing with her straightened long hair, colored streaks and twinkling eyes.

"She is my friend Simmy," Tehzeeb urged from behind. "We just met accidently at the café yesterday and shared a lot over coffee."

"Ahem! Ahem! Hi Tehzeeb!"

"Hello dear!"

"So you know each other?"

"Oh! No no…na… We actually…don't."

(To myself) Phew! Thank God!

"Excuse me Tehzeeb. I will be back in a moment. You can dance with Sid if you like!"

"I'll manage; you please carry on Dev."

Moving away from her was like moving out of a stuffy shelter into the first rains after a hot summer. But I couldn't run out of the situation. Though I was afraid of what Tehzeeb would expect next, I thought of getting back to the disc again for Tehzeeb, who might have started getting worried about me. As I opened the door to move in,

"Dev, I need you on stage, immediately…"

It was Tehzeeb on the mike.

At the sight of her only beloved (or so she thought) walking into the disc; Tehzeeb smiled and declared, "I love you Dev. I could find no better opportunity than this party to express my love for you tonight. Will you be my better half?"

The crowd went silent. People were reeling over the declaration Tehzeeb had just made in front of a whole college. In that silence however I heard the shattering of two lives clearly; the world had come to an abrupt end for Sid and Simmy. Tehzeeb's conviction of getting her beloved however never faltered. She did not hesitate in expressing herself; it was deep rooted in her to get what she desired for, by any possible means. She belonged to a well-to-do family where the stubborn daughter could demand the moon be brought to her, and her wish would be fulfilled. At that moment however, I pitied the poor father of the only girl child. Who could have imagined that the epitome of the kindness and affection that the father gave his daughter would have such results?

"I hope that our love is painted with colors not yet known to the human eye; I wish that it is chastised by the fragrance of a flower yet to be discovered and I desire that it is flavored by the taste of an exotic fruit not yet fathomed by the human tongue," she said this and ran straight towards me. I wondered what was cooking in the chain smoker's mind.

She gave me a tight hug as I saw Sid leave the party followed by Simmy, back to back. Now what could I possibly do? I was in a huge dilemma. I took the bottle of coke and smashed it on the floor, trying to vent out all the frustration and helplessness I felt; caught in the web of a friend, the one I desired and the one who desired me. Tehzeeb did not understand an inch of how I was feeling at that point of time.

"Dev, these aren't happy tears. I love you. Do you do? Today, now, here, in front of everyone, you have to tell me."

"I do. But I love somebody else. And it is my mother; more than anybody."

"Oh! That's it?" Everybody in the radius of a meter who heard this laughed at us heartily.

"You stupid fool!"

"Yes! I am. For the bottle I broke."

"No. They were empty. That's ok."

"I am not feeling the same as you do. Can we talk about this tomorrow?"

Tehzeeb was surprised to hear what I had just said; but I took no second chances and walked away from the din immediately.

I could not say anything in front of the crowd of 250 that had stood watching the drama of our real lives; all thanks to Tehzeeb. On reaching the hostel I found the room empty. "Where is Sid?" I wondered; but then suddenly sleep took over my senses and I drew it around me like a protective blanket of peace, with just a little doubt lingering inside me as I lay on my bed in the merciful dark, "Was there a need to get back to the disc?"

A week passed by and there was no sight of Sid. I too avoided classes and left the campus to spend most of my time in a lodge. I was completely screwed up. The next Monday morning as I headed towards the campus, thoughts were causing a whirlwind within my brain. I was smitten by the fear of facing Tehzeeb. Suddenly, the night watchman came and handed over an envelope to me. I thought it must be a notice, but this didn't look like one. The paper was handmade with a silken thread tied around it. I opened it to read the following:

Dear Dev,

Hope you have settled everything out for yourself by now. I just wanted to thank you for that beautiful night. You really were an angel who saved me from falling into an abyss. You came into my life, washing over me like the waves; you made me feel so utterly happy at how flawless the three months of our fantasy were turning out to be, and suddenly, without any inkling, you left me like a tide to return back to the ocean. You have left me overwhelmed with nothing but fear, sadness and pain.

You danced the entire fresher's with Tehzeeb. I knew you were going out with her, but something inside me did not want to believe this. I never knew what love was, I never believed in love until I met you. There is just one question that will always stay with me.

Why did you break my heart?

Why did you shatter my hopes & dreams? Why? Why?!! I just want to know why.

I mean you told me that you would 'die' for me.

Did you not even think, for a second, how I would be feeling as

I watched you with Tehzeeb?

How I would feel? It was all one little joke for you, wasn't it?

Ha ha... very funny indeed, I'm probably the biggest joke of your life. I bet you had a nice laugh as you sat alone on your bed that night, you sadist! You hurt me so bad, a part of me died; but if it hadn't been for you I would never have known how beautiful love can be and what bastards some people turn out to be. Thanks for educating me and making me learn a bitter lesson in life.

Seek the path of truth Dev. See what wonders life brings to you. If you really love Tehzeeb, speak the truth out and strengthen the basis of your relation with her.

Moving away from your life. Take care!

Luv, Simmy

I rushed to the reception and bribing the corrupted peon's pocket, (he had the address of every chic in the hostel) I got a piece of paper with Simmy's address on it. It was somewhere in Gandhinagar, the capital of Gujarat. On reaching the destination, I peeped inside the house but not a soul could be found. The big gate was locked with an antique piece of wood. A big garden where her black Activa should have been parked lazily, was also absent. The atmosphere was all gloomy there and the place seemed forlorn. A man in khaki with a curled up moustache came up to me.

"What do you want?"

"Does this house belong to the D' Souzas?" I fumbled looking at his intimidating posture.

"They just left the day before yesterday," he said and got back to his job.

The consequences of my first lie ever had hit me bad. I now searched for 'My experiments with truth' on the library shelves under the section tagged as Literature. I found it on the 'Grasp more' shelf.

7

This was the day all things magical and beautiful died.

That day all hopes and dreams faded into a cloudy mist of gray. That day, the meaning of joy and happiness vanished from my mind and the voids were filled with fear and pain. The day was a curse to me; maybe coz nothing was on my side.

The moment I got up in the morning, listlessness and lethargy caught up with me. My only thought that worried me was that Tehzeeb was continuously thinking about me. The only difference in our thoughts was that while I worried about the current state of affairs in my life; she had love painted all over her world. I could only satisfy Tehzeeb's obsession that day by uttering three very irrational words which meant the world to her; 'I love you'. But I had made up my mind. All I needed now was the courage to speak the truth and free myself from the abyss.

Trust and faith is what keeps every human going. The trust that one human has in another doesn't break easily; but when it does you wouldn't be able to count the shattered pieces. I was afraid and scared too. I was waiting for that one miracle that would help me retrace my steps back into the past and make me change all my misdeeds.

Finally making up my mind, I quickly got up and sent a message to Tehzeeb. "I think we should…you know… call it off."

Outraged after reading the message, her mind had a blackout. She still couldn't believe what she had just read.

"I don't get it; what happened to you all of a sudden?" She questioned me. She called on my number, but some unknown force had taken over me; I didn't respond to any of her calls and texts.

I was surprising myself by this recent behavior of mine; it just wasn't the way I generally let everything settle. Keeping myself cool I messaged her again. "Sorry. Meet me at the Crossword station. I have something important to speak to you."

"Are you going to propose me again?" was her reply and I had no words to text her back.

I wondered about the message I had sent her. What was that 'important thing' that I would be discussing with Tehzeeb? What would I say to her? That the person she loved was a fake and what had actually happened was a creation of selfish human emotions? I didn't, at any point of time wish to intentionally break her heart. Things like these kept bugging me in my head and with no warning, I suddenly became tearful; but a beep from that non-living gadget broke my woeful trance. The message read, "I'm at the Crossword store waiting for you at our favorite table. Hope you are coming?" The text got me up on my toes in an instant, as if somebody had just turned on my knob.

"Where are you?" I called up Tehzeeb on reaching our favorite place.

"Look around. Just next to your heart," she said. I thought she was fooling around as usual. I looked everywhere yet I couldn't see her; but when I turned around, to my surprise she was standing behind me in a corner.

She let out a loud laugh at being caught and I found I had a smirk on my face too; but I returned to my serious face again. I was broken, how could I laugh?

As I walked up to her, she made it look like I was a hot chocolate brownie she was waiting to devour. I just stared at her beautiful face; then immediately dropped my gaze and sternly said, "Don't look at me like that."

She knew something was wrong as I had never spoken to her like that. "What's the problem with you Dev?" She shouted exercising all her vocal chords. I turned my back to her and started walking, but she suddenly said, "Wait right there!" and we went out of the book store together. She firmly gripped on to both my hands; it was a beautiful moment that we shared whilst the wind gently swayed past us, making us feel like we were the only people in existence. But I broke that trance suddenly when I made my final decision of speaking the truth to her.

"Tehzeeb, I think we should break up," I said quietly looking down at my feet. I didn't have the guts to face her. Dropping her hands I said, "I don't love you anymore."

"What?" Her eye balls bulged as she took in what I had just said.

Her mouth fell wide open. For a moment she thought I might be kidding but then she gauged the gravity of the situation, looking at the seriousness painted all over my face.

"I can't help myself hurting you today," I said. "I am only helping you for your future. I'm trying to correct the wrongs I have done in the past. I am sure this is the right decision for you and me."

"Us being together is the right decision. This is what I want. Don't you know I want you and only you? Don't you know I love you and only you?" she responded vehemently.

"You're driving me crazy!" I had had enough of her persuasions. I couldn't take it anymore. "You're being too possessive, over protective and you don't let me do anything, don't even let me breathe alone. I need more time, more space. Will you please give that to me? I can't believe I need to beg for space and time of MY life from you. Can we please take a break? I need to think." I took a deep breath after speaking my mind out. That was all I could lie to make things look real; but things took a more violent turn and she only ended up screaming at me.

"Is that all this is about? Me being too 'possessive' and 'overprotective'? I just wanted you to be happy. I thought doing these things would make you happy," she said and tears welled up in her eyes.

"You're beautiful to my eyes; but I wasn't, I really wasn't your kind," I said and then the words stopped flowing out. We hadn't spoken to each other much in this context and just as I was about to say something she interrupted asking, "Do you love me?"

There was a long pause of a minute or so where I gasped, stopped and stared, with no emotion at all. I let go off her hands & then slowly shook my head in disapproval. She understood her beloved's non-verbal expression. That simple 'no' felt like I had killed the love and affection she had showered on me in a matter of seconds. Her world came to a halt; there were tears flowing down her cheeks, but she kept a smile on her face and turned around.

"I never loved you Tehzeeb. The only reason I was with you was to drag you away from Sid. He was spoiling his life and your life too."

"If that was the intention you could have told me. Why are you making such a fuss about this now?

"I'm sorry," I sighed. She burst into tears. "Why should we break up? I loved you, I still love you. We are perfect, we really are! But now…"

"Listen to me Tehzeeb," I held her cheeks for the last time probably. I dragged her closer and then whispered, "Everything happens for a reason. Things go wrong but, they also need to be mended eventually. Some day you will find your love. Please let go off all this pointless drama because life's too short to be anything but happy".

I turned to move out of her life forever.

"They say we don't know what we've got until we lose it, but that's not true because I know I'll always have you. No matter what people say we have to be who we are and say what we feel because life goes on. Some people may leave, some will stay; but what lingers forever is the memory we have created with each of them."

I stole one last kiss and rushed away from her to catch an auto. I had spoken to her honestly for the first time and now didn't have the guts to keep the conversation going on. She was heartbroken but what kept me steady was the thought that she will laugh again someday, dance in the rain like crazy, forgive people like me who have tried to hurt her because that was all in her past, and she knew how to move on.

It had been two days since I had seen anybody except Sid. I had slept like a little baby in my hostel room. Poor health was a strong excuse to hide all my oddities. The morning was spent lamenting. I looked around my room and just sighed. I got up out of my bed, straight away had a shower and changed into some denim jeans and a white Levi's shirt. My phone started ringing. I was in a hurry so didn't bother to look at the caller's ID. I was going to leave for class, but the person had no plans of giving up so I picked up.

It was her voice.

Tehzeeb's soft voice with loads of pain embedded in every word that she formed in her sentence. The best part of our relationship was when you said, "I'll always be there to catch you, whenever you fall. Today when that time has come, when I am falling into the shadows, I can't find you Dev."

"Wha…t?" I stammered in shock.

I couldn't comprehend anything. Suddenly she said, "Forget it, remember that I will always love you," and cut the phone. She didn't give me a second to think about what she had just said; I heard a loud blast from the grounds.

Oh my God..! My mouth fell open when I found her splayed on the ground. The blood was gushing out. It painted the ground red spreading fear and anxiety in the crowd that watched.

My hands shivered and fear ran all over my body. I had a strange, tingly feeling that started at the back of my neck. I rushed to the grounds with my feet running as fast as they could; I am sure if I was a CWG player, India would have been proud of me that day. I couldn't breathe, my heart had stopped beating; yet I ran like a leopard.

I felt so lumpy and hazardous, so freaking uncomfortable; I

wanted to jump out of my own skin if there was a choice.

I looked at Tehzeeb lying over the floor. I lifted by her arms to wake her up, crying for the lost life if god could return the soul back. I shook her, slapped her but nothing worked against the will of God.

"Call an ambulance!" I screamed at the top of my voice.

The ambulance came in time. They took her to the nearby hospital giving us no hope of her survival. Everybody rushed behind the ambulance. On the way to the hospital I kept thinking....

If only I had stopped her...

If only I had called out to her...

This...wouldn't have happened.

By the time we got to the hospital, Tehzeeb was rushed to the emergency room. She seemed to have lost a lot of blood. If she didn't get a transfusion she would surely die. Having known this, I rushed to check my blood group. Miraculously, we had the same blood group, B+. I lay down on the blood donating chamber's bed. I felt as if I was in a dark closet, a frightening closet; I imagined the walls squeezing in, choking me and smothering me.

For the first time in two years I felt like smoking to keep my mind off from what had just happened. I tried to close my eyes, but every time I did all I could remember was her face with the blood all over. It was a terrible image my mind couldn't get rid of.

I shook my head and sat up. Tears were welling up in my eyes and I hated it. Men don't cry, I reminded myself. But the tears just didn't listen to me.

My eyes wandered from one corner of the room to the other and noticed that the nurse had left with my donated blood. I took this chance to sneak out and visit Tehzeeb's room. The moment I stepped out of the room, my world began to spin. The white walls and the smell of the disinfectant made it worse.

"What the hell was that...?" I whispered to myself. I continued to walk the white wide corridors of the hospital. Around the corner from where I was, I noticed two people standing in front of the operation theatre. They were talking to each other, peering into the room where Tehzeeb was. I asked them if they would allow me to see her but they refused. The doctors were operating on her, they said.

"Such a cruel death to end the life of such a beautiful girl? God isn't always just," the guy said with a saddened tone. His gaze was cold and serious. I experienced a creepy feeling as I heard this.

The woman answered firmly, "It's as if she was a victim of somebody's cruel intentions. All that's left now is to see what happens next."

I pinched myself, "I'm awake. This is not a dream." I reminded myself.

"Hope it would have been a dream for these things wouldn't have happened!" an angry voice spoke from behind. It was Sid who had come along with Sheena, Ritesh and a few more from the college. They too were shocked on hearing the sudden news of what had just happened. Sid looked into the room and saw Tehzeeb's body through the glass window. He couldn't believe that she was in such a pathetic state. Though the doctors were doing their job; it still required a miracle to save her.

The doctors came out. They had failure written all over their faces. The only thing they could do was shake their heads from left to right.

Sid's hesitations burst out in the form of cries. He looked at me with surprised eyes and collapsed on the floor. He couldn't get words out of his mouth, but his eyes said it all.

What made everybody's heads turn was a single statement by the doctors when they disclosed the postmortem reports which said that Tehzeeb had been pregnant.

"Shhhh don't cry, please Sid… don't cry." I made Sid stand up and hugged him tight while the rest covered the two of us in a circle. Our silence was louder than the tears we tried crying for Tehzeeb and our hearts weighed heavy with the loss of a cherished one.

It was tough to handle Sid, so Sheena and Ritesh took him back to our den.

Soon the professors and other authorities of IMS arrived; but it was too late already for anyone to do anything. The only thing they could do was to inform this bad news to Tehzeeb's parents.

The police came to investigate the whole issue. I spoke to them silently and closed the case with an under table brownie that would take care of things.

The reason behind why Tehzeeb had committed suicide was a mystery to everybody, except me. But I had lost faith in me. What would I have probably said to the police? That I had messed up with that sweet girl who now happened to have a part of me inside her, which I would be obliged to babysit for the rest of my life just because the chocolate umbrella I used failed to serve the purpose? No, I couldn't see myself having the guts to say that out loud.

I stood in front of Tehzeeb's grave. The wind blew gently, sweeping the dried and withered leaves of the *Peepal* tree nearby, on to her grave, making a respectful carpet for a girl who deserved much more. I found my thoughts drifting away from the grave. I was leaving the cemetery. As soon as I passed the gate to the road out there, a very meek and aged man approached me. He was dressed in green robes of cotton.

He said in his coarse voice, "Look here!"

He seemed to have escaped out of a nearby mental hospital near the old city gate that bears the capital's name. But soon his eyes spoke of his resonance and his voice was giving me a hope that made me question my resolute and stubborn lifestyle and my ways of believing.

"Listen to me. She loved you, but remember, she still loves you. She still loves you. I know and you also know. She knows you. She ... I know you. But she still loves you. She loved you, anyway. I am hungry; pay me." He showed me his dried piece of Indian bread and a steel glass that was empty.

I was completely blank and I had nothing to doubt. The words he spoke were absolutely true. Then again, a bout of guilt haunted me. Her love and this old man reinstated the fact that I couldn't have done this.

"*Fakir, Fakir...Fakir baba*, take this money!" I shouted turning back to that man.

"No! You go, I can manage. I have a house. I don't want your money. She will meet you soon!"

"Who?"

"She may be dead but... she loves you and she will save you; may be later, but soon in life because she loves you. She still loves you."

"You have to pay... We all have to pay and bear our consequences over here only. On this very earth, he is seeing us from above. He is there right above you and when you look up at the heavens, he will show her to you! She loved you and she still loves you."

He left like a sniffer dog eager to catch another culprit like me. I had never in life seen people having an extra perception of things like the Fakir. I had seen Medusa's touch and other horror movies, but when it happened in front of my own eyes, it seemed pretty horrifying. In some weird way though, it pacified the troubled lover in me.

My legs were moving normally. No one knew what happened that day; neither the leaves, nor the old man, nor you, nor me. But everything, everyone anticipated the phenomenal storm that was about to take place that night.

As I reached my hostel, Sid was shaking badly. I turned the lights on. I tried calming Sid down, but it was difficult to pacify him. Somehow he had convinced himself to accept the fact that Tehzeeb was dead; but he couldn't help feeling empty. There are some things that don't change and some things which take time to accept.

I gave Sid sleeping pills to settle his thoughts down.

I noticed the blood spots on my white Levi's shirt as I did so. I felt like a murderer; a killer who had just taken a life. I could only curse myself because I knew that in hell I was answerable to God before I surrendered my soul.

I undressed keeping all ill thoughts aside and hit the shower. The smell of blood began to fade and I felt refreshed. Yet every time I closed my eyes, all I could remember was her face. How could I forget her face? How could I forget her eyes? That was the first and last time I'd see that lifeless stony expression on her.

The room's temperature was dropping and fear began to seep into me. Her voice in my head became clearer now; I could hear it distinctly as the world around me muted itself. I took two steps away from the window and turned to my right. My eyes caught the glimpse of a shadow taking form on the wall. The mist was drawn by its presence and it slowly embodied the shadow. My senses began to tingle with fear and excitement of some unknown kind.

Is this her ghost? Is she haunting me? Why me?

I backed up to the wall as the image became clearer. It was her. It was Tehzeeb. I could recognize that smile. There was no mistake. Her soul was in my room and I got as frightened as a mouse in front of a hungry cat. I began to tremble; I figured out that she must be here for revenge. My knees gave way and my body sat trembling in the dark. All I could do was sit at the corner and stare.

"I'm sorry Tehzeeb, please don't kill me," I said stammering with sweat all over my face.

"I'm neither here to kill you, nor would I take any revenge," a soft whisper echoed in the room.

"Then why are you here? You want my life too...?" I shouted angrily.

The voice was making me insane. I thought of taking the same sleeping pills which I had given Sid; it would surely ease the pressure inside my brain. I checked Sid's wardrobe for extra pills but found nothing except clothes. Suddenly, as I was about to shut the cabinet door, my eyes caught sight of a strange substance dangling out of his bag.

"Oh my God!" I whispered into the open wardrobe. I was shocked when I reached out and found a white powder packet inside Sid's bag. Was he taking drugs? I questioned myself. But right now, what I needed more than anything else was a sedative; something that could take me away from reality even if it was for a minute. Tehzeeb's voice was driving me insane.

I locked myself up in the bathroom of my room. I took a small glass and filled it up with water. I took the packet out and added a few grams to the glass dissolving it in the water. My whole body was practically quivering with anticipation; maybe because I wanted the drug so badly right now. I was dealing with too much of pain and I couldn't carry the burden; I couldn't take it anymore.

I pressed Sid's lighter for the flame. I flamed the coke lightly over the glass until the liquid began to bubble and white wisps of smoke rose up. Breaking off a small piece of cotton from the cotton ball, I pulled the plunger from the syringe as the liquid filled in.

I tied my handkerchief to my upper arm, making a fist and watched the bluish green veins pop up.

The needle pierced my skin effortlessly; then without thinking too much, I pushed the plunger and watched the liquid disappear.

I began to cough and choke, my head throbbing with the worst headache I've ever had till date. My breathing quickened, I gasped and yearned for the air that refused to reach my lungs; my eyes watered and everything blurred before my eyes as I dipped out of the real world.

In a matter of minutes everything changed; an overwhelming sense of happiness that I had not felt in months took over my body.

"Dev! Are you ok?" yelled Sid pounding his fist on the door. He banged the door a zillion times but did not get any response.

Finally he broke the door and dashed into the bathroom.

I woke up with a splitting headache; the world around me still a little tipsy. If you've never had a hangover before, let me tell you what it feels like. If someone took a hammer and slammed it on your head umpteen times, how would your poor body react? Nauseous and unbalanced for an entire day would be my closest answer.

When I finally managed to retch out all the toxic contents of my stomach, Sid gave me a glass of water to hydrate myself. I was still sick and my head was throbbing like hell. He picked me up from the bathroom floor, made me lie down on the bed and covered me up.

He then picked up my clothes and handed them over to me. "Are you alright?" he asked looking genuinely concerned. I looked at him with a few tears trickling down my cheeks and nodded. He heaved a huge sigh of relief and proceeded to leave the room.

"I'm going to run to the Mc Donald's outlet nearby to get you something to eat. It'll help you. Here's some water if you need it when I am gone; just rest for some time now," he said with a dismal look on his face. He locked the door when he left, just in case someone happened to pry.

I sat there frozen and ashamed of myself. How did I get myself into this problematic mess? I waited for Sid to come back but hours passed away and there was no sign of him. I checked his wardrobe and it was empty. He had gone far away from me, never to return back.

My eyes must have reflected the sadness I was inflicted with, for Dr. Astha put a consoling hand on my shoulder, asking me to drop the guilt I bore for the mistakes I had committed.

"So tell me Doctor was I a friend or a foe to him? How do I make him see the truth that while I was with Tehzeeb I was serving a purpose, the purpose of a true friend?" I said.

"At the cost of somebody's life," she reminded me with disdain.

"But how do I get out of my past, rid myself of the demons that haunt me and revert back to my old self? I forced the questions away from my mind but they chase me for the answers."

"It has indeed been painful for you," she spoke solemnly looking at me.

"Sometimes in life, you do not understand what to do and so you end up making mistakes. I thought I could show him the truth, and explain why I did what I did. But when I saw Sid enjoying

Tehzeeb's company which he had always wanted, I should have left him all alone with the girl. That's where I went wrong. I shouldn't have messed up everything like this and so I have paid heavily for it.

I tried to escape; but the web I'm caught in, only entangled me further.

These days I have forgotten how to be myself; I left my soul to be driven away by scrupulous thoughts and now I am suffering as there is nowhere I can look for the reason of my actions. Why did I do all this, things that can never be undone, words that can never be taken back? All this while I assumed my conscience to be clear; but when I realized how deeply I had affected and hurt another human being's feelings in the name of friendship, my conscience ceased to remain clear. How now will this boy who walked into IMS from a small town of Nadiad face himself in the mirror?"

I looked back at Dr. Astha. She knew that I was probably scared. She stood in front of me with a smile. "Its okay, Sid will be fine."

Those were the exact words that I wanted to hear from her. It gave me a great sense of comfort. It boosted my courage to face reality, a reality that I had been running away from.

"Though I have lost my friend, deep inside my heart she will always stay alive," I said.

Just then a compounder arrived yelling, "Doctor… Doctor Astha!

The patient in ward no. 104 has regained consciousness. He is gasping for breath!"

"Let's go," Dr. Astha gestured to follow as she rushed to the ward. As we reached the ward I saw Sid. His eyes were puffy and his heart was thumping; I could hear his every heartbeat. Dr. Astha checked his pulse.

"Dev – oh! That's good news," she said as she checked the cardiogram. "Look at this, his heart beat is normal. He will be fine, don't worry. Let me examine his pressure."

I was more than happy to hear this news. I was happy for Sid and I thought I could finally rectify my mistakes. Dr. Astha left the room to attend to some other casualties leaving Sid and me alone. I raised Sid's hand and held it with both of mine.

"I'm extremely sorry Sid," I burst out loudly as he saw me. For the first time I was so ashamed that I couldn't even meet his eyes. They were filled with questions; questions waiting to be asked. All I could do was gather enough guts to speak the truth to Sid; maybe that would free me from all the burdens I was carrying? I took a deep breath and began speaking.

"Siddy, your name seems immortal to me. You were and are the only friend I have and when it came to friendship I thought I could do better for you. Your obsession towards Tehzeeb was driving me crazy. It always made me wonder that it might hurt you a lot if she said, 'No'. I played with human emotions and never thought this could hurt so many lives. That time I wasn't aware of the consequences of my little plan that I hatched when you went to your orphanage. I wish I had not interfered in your affairs, spoiling all of our lives in a jiffy. I'm feeling ashamed to be called your friend now for the mistakes that I have committed. The only thing that stuck with me was your sentence, "I will leave my obsession for Tehzeeb if she finds somebody else."

I slapped myself many times with both my hands when I confessed to Sid that the unborn life inside Tehzeeb was mine. Sid, for the first time felt like saying something to me after he'd deserted me in the hostel room. He took out his mask and tried to mutter that dark fact that was clawing his insides. I was craving for the words to spill out of his mouth; those words of anger, hatred and anguish which would settle all my guilt.

"Tehzeeb died.... The... hh... zeeb...." He was not able to speak as he was wheezing. I was just crying not even listening to him, but again he tried hard, "Tehzeeb... died," he stammered.

"I know Sid, please calm down... Doctor... Doctor," I shouted as I found Sid gasping for his breath. I felt as if he had wanted to say something more, but to my horror he stopped mid sentence. The shock of what was happening to Sid made me revisit the guilt lane. It was a whirlwind coming my way and I couldn't escape from getting devastated by it.

Sid kept his eyes wide open staring at me. I needed him to blink; but he didn't. I cried for the Doctor, for Sid and for everything.

"Dr. Astha! Look at him. Why isn't he responding? What has happened to him? Please do something!" I pleaded. She began working on Sid as quickly as the questions that I threw at her.

I was afraid of what the future had in store for me; but I didn't have to wait for too long. Reality came charging at me with such gusto; I was knocked out cold.

"I'm sorry… he is no more," Dr. Astha said as she walked out of the room. I shook my head. It was easier to believe that Dr. Astha had made a mistake. I checked his pulse; nothing could be heard.

All I could do was 'think'! Think about what could've happened if I had done the right thing or had made the right decision. If I had known of this future what would I have done to have it changed?

Questions rapidly filled my mind just like an outrageous sea that fills up the coasts during a Tsunami. There were so many things unknown to me. They were questions that required an abundant amount of thought that made me come out of my comfort zone and relive past events that were better left forgotten!

Reality bites were tough to bear. I became the rotten apple for many in the college. I was left alone, ignored as a rabid dog, after the trio left my life. Even Sheena and Ritesh saw me guilty, leaving me to bear what was written in my fate alone. They started maintaining distance from me, for they knew about my plight with Tehzeeb. Whom all could I convince now and try to befriend? I was so lonely, as Akon sings in his song.

I hardly had any good memories that persisted in my head for long enough.

I went from being an above average student in class to a barely passing student in a matter of days. I started doing things I never thought I would do before; bullying students and fighting without reason just because someone looked at me in the wrong way. My friends Sheena and Ritesh had parted ways with me. They thought I had done wrong to that girl. I rarely smiled now. I was always moody and angry with my friends and my teachers. I began to skip college and no one seemed to care, so I was soon absent nearly every day.

I settled myself inside my dorm till the final exams.

The last few embers of my life glowed at the ends of the cigarettes I smoked. I held it just above the ashtray, overflowing with butts and loose tobacco which had spilled out from the cracks where the paper had not been properly sealed. As the paper started to burn and crackle, I lifted the short and thick cigarette up to my mouth, held it to my pursed lips, and dragged hard, making the nicotine burn quickly as air passed through it and the smoke devoured my lungs.

I watched the dim light that glowed in the centre of my room, and tried to see the cream ceiling through the thick smoke that I now sat in. This had become a routine with every joint I smoked.

I watched the swirling patterns of the smoke, tried to imagine images forming in front of me. Those images of Sid and Tehzeeb in the smoke drove me crazy.

Their thoughts haunted me, horrified me at nights. Somehow I managed to pass the semester, in spite of all the lack of concentration that I suffered from.

Dad was happy to see me at the convocation. He came along with all my family and friends to share the happiness of my graduation day and take me home. He was more than happy on hearing from me that I would continue with him in our family business.

At home, a weird numbness settled over me, distancing me from everything in this world. Some people like it; others don't. For me it was a way of life. Drugs and cigarettes became a necessity that kept me alive and without them, I would feel lost.

I started stealing money from my parents and I lied to other people just to get some money for drugs. After my parents found me stealing their money, they got angry with me.

A few months later, I was tired of everything I was doing and wanted to quit this kind of life. I wanted to go back to being the person I had been before. I asked my parents to take me to any drug rehabilitation clinic they knew of. They agreed and helped me out without getting angry. They supported me and helped me to quit drugs. They first took me to a hospital to get a therapy done, but it didn't work. I came back and started taking drugs again. Then they took me to a drug rehabilitation program in another province. But only after a few days of staying there; I ran away.

They took me to a few more places; but each time I came back I became more addicted to drugs. I also started experimenting with other varieties of drugs that I hadn't tried before. My parents tried helping me loads of times; but they finally gave up on me when I started stealing from them again.

After that they never trusted or believed in anything I said to them. They said to me that they couldn't help me if I didn't want to help myself. They stopped giving me money and locked up everything inside the house that could be stolen. The condition worsened to an extent where they didn't trust me even if I asked them for twenty bucks to eat a meal outside. They didn't give it to me because they thought I was lying to them and wanted the money for drugs.

Still Tehzeeb's voice echoed in my ears. I was lost. Not lost; just dead. I had tried to commit suicide; but I knew I couldn't. I used to have feelings a very long time ago, but something happened that changed everything, turned everything upside down. It unleashed a pain like none other I had experienced before. A pain so excruciating that it hurt to smile, to breath, to live. I wanted to die. I tried to end my meaningless life but after a few failed attempts, I gave up. Instead, I found something else; a cure. It took the horrible pain away and replaced it with nothingness; an empty space inside my mind, body and soul. I was empty and it is the best choice I have ever made.

Epilogue

"God has given us only one life and it's our duty to cherish it, value it and make the most of it. You are the master of a healthy body and a sound mind and it is just not worth it to throw it away on any kind of addiction.

Today there are quite a large number of people who can be seen becoming addicts to alcohol, drugs, sex or anything which can create a negative effect on your body. Look at me now; do you know how I was? And now how do you think I am? I had no good memories, had lost all my friends, had parted from my family and that one important thing – 'Love' had vanished from my life completely.

Tell me have you ever been in love?

I had. They were the best friends I ever had and today I realize what I have lost. On losing them I felt like I had lost all the good I had in me. But if I told you it was the most amazing feeling in this world, I guess I'd be lying. My world shattered as I lost them because of my mistakes. With love, not only does the feeling of amazement and wonder come; but the feeling of being desperate, sad and hurt finds its way into us too. It's been four years and I still crave for their love.

I knew somewhere at the back of my mind that I'd lost them forever; but a guy can still hope, right?"

"Right!" The audience echoed back.

"Every night they came in my dreams. But that night when Sid came, he told me how worried he was for me. He said he didn't like the way things were turning out for me and that he wanted something better for me because even in death he loved me and has watched over me from above ever since. I woke up speechless and broke into a cold sweat. My heart seemed to be pumping a million times per minute. I suddenly felt stale and decayed. That's when I decided to come out of my dingy shell, for Sid had shown me the path to recovery; he had shown me light. The journey since then has not been a smooth ride; believe me, it is only raw determination and will power that keeps me going. But I know where I am heading towards, for the first time in my life.

Now I know what defines me; someone who isn't going to be addicted anymore. My name is Devendra Rai and I'm a recovering addict."

There was a huge round of applause from the participants sitting in the audience while one lady whispered to another, "That was Dev. He is currently assisting the victims of the slow poison at a rehab in Ahmedabad. He too was a victim and stayed in rehabilitation for four long years before turning into a new leaf. The change that has taken over him is overwhelming. You should have seen his state before. It seemed like he would never come out. But look at him now, what a drastic change in his appearance! He is now neat and clean with a military cut that suits his twisted skull. His attire and gait have changed too and he now reflects the seriousness of a corporate employee."

Suddenly a sweet little girl of three appeared in front of Dev, making him wonder what had brought her to a rehab centre.

"Hello *beta*! What's your name?" Dev asked. The other participants had just left and it was only him and that toddler inside the room.

"Guddiya," she said while prancing all over the room.

"Guddiya! Who brought you here?" Somehow she resembled Simmy. Dev's heart started pounding and he went cold again. His senses signalled him that somebody very close to him was nearby. As he turned back to look beyond the door his heart raced faster. He waited for that somebody to push the door and come inside. Seconds passed and there still wasn't a mortal in sight.

He dropped his gaze and turned back to Guddiya who was playing in her own world. Then suddenly, Dev looked up and skipped a heartbeat, as Simmy walked in looking for someone.

"Guddiya, are you there?" She shouted while making her way inside the room; she stopped when she saw Dev.

For a moment she was mum as if the world around her has yet again turned unstable. They didn't realize how long they stood there in front of each other. What would she probably have said or asked? There were no hopes, no thoughts and maybe there were no feeling.

They couldn't meet each others' eyes for all that had passed between them; they kept staring at the floor nevertheless. Dev finally made a start, realizing that they have been standing silent for too long.

"Is she you daughter?" the first stupid question.

"Yes," she said.

"How come you are here?"

"A friend of mine is employed here. Do you know Dr. Sabrina?"

"Oh! Miss *Batliwala*? Yes... yes, how can I forget that sweet lady? It was she who treated me."

"What kind of treatment?" she asked.

"I'm not a part of this rehab program. I'm a patient here"

"How come?" She stammered partly out of shock and partly

out of how absurd the whole thing sounded. She couldn't digest the fact that I had become an addict.

"It's a long story," I sighed. "But meanwhile, where have you been? I tried to contact you, reach you through your neighbours. The first few months I talked to them and used to ask about you. But for some crazy, wild reason they never replied or picked up any phone calls after the sixth month. I wondered why and I still do. Even after I knew that they wouldn't pick up, I'd still call every once in a while hoping that you will come back."

"Come back for what Dev? That day at the fresher's I was heartbroken and couldn't digest the fact that you were playing with me. My world had come to an end and I pushed myself to commit that blunder named suicide. It was insane. Dad took me far away from your shadow and I gradually found it easier to live. It was difficult at the beginning; then life took a new turn, and a happier one surely, when i got married to Ranbir Singh, an NRI from Boston. He is really a sweetheart and trusts me; I'm happy with him."

"I never thought after parting ways that we would meet this way."

"Life plays many games with us and this is one amongst many. After you went, Tehzeeb committed suicide. Your departure taught me the necessity of speaking the truth and I adopted the Gandhian path. I was the reason behind her death, but I never knew that my actions would have had such an adverse effect on Sid too. He was obsessed with Tehzeeb and her sudden death drained the joy out of him. His life went stale like a rotten apple and he got infected with drug addiction. I couldn't sleep since their deaths. I never knew life would make me walk on Sid's path to destruction. So here I am in front of you struggling from all the odds of my past for a better future."

"I feel sorry about Tehzeeb; didn't think she would end her life this way," she said looking into my eyes. She took out a letter from her bag and gave it to me. "Sid was really a bastard and God has punished him for his deeds."

Fumes emerged from inside me, when I heard those bitter words from her. After Sid went away from me, my life had become hell. I had lived because of him, his belief in me, his wish to see me do better in life; had it not been for him, I would have simply ended my life. His spirit had become my soul giving me enthusiasm and zest to lead a beautiful life that waited ahead for me.

Simmy didn't react to my behaviour. She knew how much I loved him; beyond imagination. No matter what other relations I had had in life, he would always be a brother to me. But I never knew what he really was, until Simmy gave me the letter to read.

My hands were shaking and my mind, spirit and body swirled when I realised that the letter was from Tehzeeb.

Hi Dev,

Ending my life is completely my decision and there is no way that you could be blamed for this. But somewhere in the corners of my heart, there are things left unsaid, questions that remained unanswered and if I don't say and ask them in this letter to you, I know I wouldn't die in peace. I want to know why you did this. Why me?

I valued every word that you had expressed from your heart. How dare you utter such sweetness and teach me the language of love when you yourself never recognized the creation of your own expressions?

You fooled me completely Dev, if that is what satisfies you and you played with my feelings; you knew I'd get my hopes high enough for I trusted you and you knew that if I fall down from that unrealistic height, I would shatter into a million pieces and I did.

Everyday my love for you grew and grew; it became so intense after a point of time that nothing could annihilate it. You told me I was perfect & beautiful in every way to you and I thought nothing could come between us and nothing did come between us.

Dev cannot do this, is what I kept thinking all the time. I wished that you'd quit playing games, quit hanging out with other women and actually whisper, 'I love you' to me when you were sober. I don't really understand how I let myself come so undone, unraveling this web that I had worked so hard to entangle myself in. My efforts were devoted to everything from tying strings to laying bricks as I built my wall, higher and higher. But the biggest lie you told me was that you loved me. It felt like embracing heaven every time I was in your arms and whenever you gave me your hand, I'd hold on to it so firmly and I'd feel like never letting you go; your warmth, your touch was just so magical, so sweet to me; you were perfect, you were flawless.

But you left me all alone. I was so mad about you, so crazy, so passionate and so fucking stupid! But this is what I get for believing in you more than I believed in love!

I will remember you for the world that I just had to dream of, from a distance.

Thank you, Dev

Luv Tehzeeb!

My hands continued shivering as I read the letter. I looked here and there to find the reason why my world was turning tipsy again.

I could hear the voices in my head again. I suddenly felt as if I could not breathe, as if my heart had stopped.

That uncomfortable feeling of being trapped in a dark closet, a dark frightening closet came back to me. I imagined the walls squeezing in, choking me and smothering me once again.

"You shouldn't have played with that girl's feelings," Simmy said consoling me.

"I never thought that one Saturday could change my life. I'm sorry Simmy," I burst out crying. All I needed was a shoulder to cry on and Simmy didn't take a moment to give me that support.

"But I couldn't help it and I still can't understand what was happening then," I said. It all started with Sid and his possessiveness. That night I had a chat with Sid who stated that if Tehzeeb fell in lovc with somebody other than him, he will throw her out of his life. I decided to end Sid's obsession with my own mind games. Everything went off smoothly. I thought that college love was a frivolous affair that would end in college itself; but I was wrong. I underestimated the supernatural powers of love that makes people so crazy. I never trusted love and never realized that love could be so dangerous. I didn't play games with you to tell you the truth Simmy, but actually life played games with me when I was introduced to you. You stole my heart and captured my emotions. I never felt so worthwhile back then. In life there is a stage when you are given an opportunity to protect and rescue your partner. Circumstances were such that I was unable to prevent my beloved from succumbing to the fate of her life. I am guilty for that. Just one lustful thought of mine triggered off this whole chain of events that has caused the destruction of so many lives, and has proven me guilty and unfaithful and worthless and God knows what else."

"It wasn't you Dev... it wasn't you who was responsible for the pregnancy," she said as she looked straight into my eyes. "I'm sorry for not telling you the truth which has been troubling my heart for the last four years. Tehzeeb made me promise that I'd keep mum, but today I feel like I owe you the truth. I still can't imagine that my silence brought you here. Sid was really a bastard."

All I could hear was my heart pumping which I was sure would fall out of my chest as I screamed to release the anger pent up inside of me.

Simmy's POV

It was two day after our fresher's party. My world had already come to an end and every minute of mine passed in depression. At that moment when the clock showed 11:48 at night I got a call. I was just not in the mood to talk to anyone. I tried to get rid of the phone, but Tehzeeb wasn't giving up. I thought I'd pick up the call and yell at that bitch.

It was unexpected to receive a call from her of all the people. I had nothing to say to her; but then I thought I'd have a word.

On picking up the phone, I found her crying. Was she hurt after discovering the fate of her life? I wondered. I was in deep shock when she told me that Sid had become aggressive and had raped her. He wasn't in his senses and his mind only bore the hurt and pain of being rejected. She had lost all her will and couldn't think of a support except me. I immediately rushed to the medical store before reaching her dorm. The store manager cast curious looks at me which I avoided, paid for my goods and scurried back to my car. As I reached her room, I saw her in a mess. She was broken and every inch of her cried. I handed over the packet to her which she tore and headed to the toilet. She was sweating. She came out carrying the strip in her hand. She sat on the couch in the living area, waiting. It took three minutes to show the result. Each second was weighing heavy for her. And the result was disastrous. The strip had turned red. Tehzeeb broke into tears. She was pregnant and alone. Nobody was there to be with her except for me. She couldn't tell you, nor could she tell this to anybody at college. I pulled her together and she cried like hell. It was difficult to accept this grim reality that she had to face. She looked at the strip again and again. Although she knew the result wouldn't change, she wished that it would...but it wouldn't. She just threw the strip in the trash bin. What could she do now? What would her father say? And the scene dissolved into several small scenes of her crying in front of me, in the shower, in the college. I never thought she would take such a drastic step. She was really a sweet girl and Sid's obsession took her life eventually."

I cried out loud on hearing Simmy. I never thought a friend like Sid could do such a thing. My love for him didn't mean anything because the possessiveness bug had infected him. I had realised how mad I was for Sid, which had made me ruin three lives. I lost all hope and became an addict, spending the rest of my years with the hope that one day I would get back again to live my life. I never thought *'The Dev-D Syndrome'* would take over me but it happened, all for my dear friend Sid.

My mind kept visualizing images of the past; how Sid had been a brother to me. I had felt a stab when the doctor had said that Tehzeeb was no more. The stab I felt had been more for how Sid would feel on knowing this, and a little less for the friend that I had just lost. I saw those tears when he broke down. For years now, I couldn't face myself in the mirror for I knew that the reason behind Tehzeeb's death had been me; the reason behind Sid's merciful fate had also me. But today when I realized that fake side of Sid's, my trust on him has come to an end. Sid collapsed because he knew what a cruel thing he'd done to that girl. He went on drugs because he couldn't stop himself from going insane. His guilt had taken over his life.

Today I came to know what he was trying to tell me. His last words revolved around Tehzeeb's death. I only heard half of his sentence, "Tehzeeb died... because of me."

I was jolted back to reality when Simmy stood up to leave.

"Dev, I respected you & I always prayed for your happiness & success; maybe that's why you're so lucky today to have met me. I loved you with all my heart and no one can ever love you more than I did. My mind was drawn to you because you were the only person who made me feel so loved. I know things would never be the same, but life is very short and I will cherish this moment here forever," she said and took Guddiya in her arms. They waved at me and departed.

It was at this moment that I knew I had to change myself. I

knew I had to start making better decisions in life.

Now that I know what defines me, someone who isn't going to be addicted anymore.